Margaret Elizabeth Munson Sangster

Poems of the Household

Margaret Elizabeth Munson Sangster

Poems of the Household

ISBN/EAN: 9783337408671

Printed in Europe, USA, Canada, Australia, Japan

Cover: Foto ©Andreas Hilbeck / pixelio.de

More available books at **www.hansebooks.com**

POEMS

OF

THE HOUSEHOLD

BY

MARGARET E. SANGSTER

BOSTON

JAMES R. OSGOOD AND COMPANY

1882

Many of these bits of verse, now gathered into a volume, originally appeared in "Harper's Monthly" and "Bazar," "The Christian Intelligencer," "Sunday-School Times," and elsewhere.

CONTENTS.

6 *Contents.*

Contents.

POEMS OF THE HOUSEHOLD.

MOTH-EATEN.

I HAD a beautiful garment
　　And I laid it by with care ;
I folded it close, with lavender leaves,
　　In a napkin fine and fair :
" It is far too costly a robe," I said,
　　" For one like me to wear."

So never at morn or evening
　　I put my garment on ;
It lay by itself, under clasp and key,
　　In the perfumed dusk alone, —
Its wonderful broidery hidden
　　Till many a day had gone.

There were guests who came to my portal,
　　There were friends who sat with me,

And clad in soberest raiment
  I bore them company ;
I knew that I owned a beautiful robe,
  Though its splendor none might see.

There were poor who stood at my portal,
  There were orphaned sought my care ;
I gave them the tenderest pity,
  But had nothing beside to spare ;
I had only the beautiful garment,
  And the raiment for daily wear.

At last, on a feast-day's coming,
  I thought in my dress to shine ;
I would please myself with the lustre
  Of its shifting colors fine ;
I would walk with pride in the marvel
  Of its rarely rich design.

So out from the dust I bore it —
  The lavender fell away —
And fold on fold I held it up
  To the searching light of day.
Alas ! the glory had perished
  While there in its place it lay.

Who seeks for fadeless beauty
   Must seek for the use that seals,
To the grace of a constant blessing,
   The beauty that use reveals,
For into the folded robe alone
   The moth with its blighting steals.

POND–LILIES.

IN early morning, when the air
　Is full of tender prophecy,
And rose-hue faint and pearl-mist fair
　Are hints of splendor yet to be,

The lilies open.　Gleaming white,
　Their fluted cups like onyx shine,
And golden-hearted, in the light,
　They hold the summer's rarest wine.

Ah, love, what mornings thou and I
　Once idly drifted through, afloat
Among the lilies, with the sky
　Cloud-curtained o'er our tiny boat !

Noon climbed apace with ardent feet ;
　The goblets shut, whose honey-dew
Was overbrimmed with subtle sweet
　While yet the silver dawn was new.

The pomp of royal crowning lay
  On daisied field and dimpling dell;
And on the blue hills far away
  In dazzling waves the glory fell;

And, flashing to our measured stroke,
  The waters seemed a path of gems,
Beneath whose clear refraction broke
  A grove with mirrored fronds and stems.

In music on the sparkling shore
  The plashing ripples fell asleep:
We laid aside the dripping oar,
  For our delight we could not keep.

In all the splendor farther on
  We missed the morning's maiden blush;
The soft expectancy was gone, —
  The brooding haze, the trembling flush.

TROUBLE.

ONE folds the little white hands, and lays a flower
between,
And sees death's lilies pale, where life's sweet rose
hath been,
And aches through all her heart beside the baby face
serene.

One smiles a brave good-morrow, and walks with even
tread,
The while she bears the burden of a great and nameless dread ;
God wot, — a living grief is worse than the peace that
folds the dead.

THE ACADEMY BELL.

THE rich air is sweet with the breath of September,
    The sumach is staining the hedges with red ;
Soft rests on the hill-slopes the light we remember,
    The glory of days which so long ago fled, —
        When, brown-cheeked and ruddy,
          Blithe-hearted and free,
        The summons to study
          We answered with glee.
Listen, oh ! listen once more to the swell
Of the masterful, merry Academy bell !

It sounds not in vain over mountain and valley,
    That tocsin which gathers the far-scattered clans ;
From playtime and leisure fleet-footed they rally,
    Brave lads and bright lasses, o'erflowing with plans ;
        From croquet and cricket
          To blackboard and map,
        Is but shooting a wicket ;
          No fear of mishap.

Oh hark ! how it echoes through dingle and dell,
The jocund, the earnest Academy bell !

They fly, at its call, from soft mother caresses ;
  The boy will not tarry, the girl cannot wait ;
So the round head close-clipped and the loose flowing
    tresses
  Together flash out from the vine-trellised gate ;
        And the house that was holden
          By revel supreme,
        Is wrapped in the golden
          Fair peace of a dream.
  To sisters and mothers how silvern the swell
Of the rest-bringing, easeful Academy bell.

The path by the river, where willows are drooping,
  Is radiant with children.   The long city street,
All busy with traffic, makes room for their trooping,
  And rings to the rush of their beautiful feet.
        For the poet and preacher,
          The man of affairs,
        And the gentle home-teacher,
          O'er-burdened with cares,
  Alike spare a moment to wishing them well,
Who speed when they hear the Academy bell.

God bless them, our darlings ! God give them full
    measure
Of joy at the fountains of wisdom and truth ;
We tenderly view the enchantment of pleasure
    Which royally lies on the days of their youth ;
        For, brown-cheeked and ruddy,
          When children at home,
        That summons to study
          Once called us to come ;
And voices departed we hear in the swell
Of the never-forgotten Academy bell.

ARE THE CHILDREN AT HOME?

EACH day when the glow of sunset
　　Fades in the western sky,
And the wee ones, tired of playing,
　　Go tripping lightly by,
I steal away from my husband,
　　Asleep in his easy-chair,
And watch from the open doorway
　　Their faces fresh and fair.

Alone in the dear old homestead,
　　That once was full of life,
Ringing with girlish laughter, —
　　Echoing boyish strife, —
We two are waiting together;
　　And oft, as the shadows come,
With tremulous voice he calls me :
　　" It is night ! are the children home?"

"Yes, love !" I answer him gently,
  "They 're all home long ago ; "
And I sing, in my quivering treble,
  A song so soft and low,
Till the old man drops to slumber,
  With his head upon his hand,
And I tell to myself the number
  Home in the Better Land.

Home, where never a sorrow
  Shall dim their eyes with tears !
Where the smile of God is on them
  Through all the summer years !
I know, — yet my arms are empty,
  That fondly folded seven,
And the mother heart within me
  Is almost starved for heaven.

Sometimes, in the dusk of evening,
  I only shut my eyes,
And the children are all about me,
  A vision from the skies :
The babes whose dimpled fingers
  Lost the way to my breast,
And the beautiful ones, the angels,
  Passed to the world of the blest.

With never a cloud upon them,
    I see their radiant brows :
My boys that I gave to freedom, —
    The red sword sealed their vows !
In a tangled Southern forest,
    Twin brothers, bold and brave
They fell ; and the flag they died for,
    Thank God ! floats over their grave.

A breath, and the vision is lifted
    Away on wings of light,
And again we two are together,
    All alone in the night.
They tell me his mind is failing,
    But I smile at idle fears ;
He is only back with the children,
    In the dear and peaceful years.

And still as the summer sunset
    Fades away in the west,
And the wee ones, tired of playing,
    Go trooping home to rest,
My husband calls from his corner :
    "Say, love ! have the children come ? "
And I answer, with eyes uplifted :
    " Yes, dear ! they are all at home ! "

BEFORE THE LEAVES FALL.

I WONDER if oak and maple,
  Willow and elm and all,
Are stirred at heart by the coming
  Of the day their leaves must fall.
Do they think of the yellow whirlwind,
  Or know of the crimson spray,
That shall be when chill November
  Bears all their leaves away?

Perhaps — beside the water
  The willow bends, serene
As when her young leaves glistened
  In a mist of golden green ;
But the brave old oak is flushing
  To a wine-red, dark and deep,
And maple and elm are blushing
  The blush of a child asleep.

" If die we must," the leaflets
   Seem one by one to say ;
" We will wear the colors of gladness
   Until we pass away.
No eyes shall see us falter ;
   And, before we lay it down,
We 'll wear, in the sight of all the earth,
   The year's most kingly crown."

So, trees of the stately forest,
   And trees by the trodden way,
You are kindling into glory
   This soft autumnal day.
And we who gaze remember
   That more than all they lost,
To hearts and trees together,
   May come through the ripening frost.

A VANISHED HOPE.

SWEET with the scents of the summer,
   White with the dew and the sun,
Wee as the robes of the fairies,
   She folded them one by one.

Royally fair was the raiment,
   Though none but herself might see
How the heart with the hand had labored
   For the Prince who was yet to be !

Into those tiny garments
   Was more than of needle wrought —
Hours of loving fancies,
   Beautiful flights of thought.

By lane and road were burning,
   In splendor of crimson dyes,
Maple and elm and sumach,
   Shaming the sunset skies.

She smiled from her chamber window :
   " Ah, fade, bright leaves ! " she said,
" For I 'll be glad with my baby,
   When all the leaves are dead ! "

Cold is the heaven above her,
   Cloudy and dark the day,
As she looks again in sorrow
   That is slow to pass away.

Useless the treasures of linen,
   And the cobweb frosts of lace ;
Her babe on mother's bosom
   Found briefest resting-place.

All night she hears the north wind,
   She feels the rain and the snow ;
Whenever they fall on her darling,
   Over her heart they go.

Sleep hath no fetter to bind her,
　Ever its spell will break ;
At the dream of a touch like a roseleaf,
　The grief returns to ache.

Comfort her not with the angels,
　Since — changing her day to night —
Some pitiless angel carried
　Her firstborn out of her sight !

LOVE-LORN.

IN her cage by my window swings a bird,
   A beautiful bird with golden wing,
And all day long, by a memory stirred,
   In a faint little treble she tries to sing.

I list to the twitter, so soft and low,
   To the quavering trill that breaks in twain;
The silver song she recalls, I know, —
   The song she tries to repeat in vain.

In April days of the budding leaves
   A mate was hers, with a tuneful breast;
But the summer long, to the time of sheaves,
   She was all alone in the tiny nest.

And in and out, through the peace profound
　　Of the silent, slumberous, summer noon, —
A tremulous, touching, pathetic sound, —
　　She wove the thought of a transient tune.

The jar-fly broke with his cadenced whir,
　　A comma of sound in a silent space ;
The south wind moved with a gentle stir
　　Through the shadowy leaves of his hiding-place.

The lilies stood in their vestal robes,
　　White as a nun's, by the garden gate ;
And, light as a feather-puff, the globes
　　Of the thistle rose at the waft of fate.

Still feebly rippled across the air
　　The low love-note of a vanished song, —
The moan of a hopeless, desolate prayer, —
　　Till the days grew short and the nights grew long.

" O Bird, my Bird, you never were meant
　　To warble songs for the world to hear !
You were made for the stillness of shy content,
　　And the quiet round of a homely sphere ;

" For the patient waiting of brooding days,
   And the overflood of a mother's heart ;
For tender pride in the winning ways
   Of your wee ones dear, from the world apart.

" And why, in a rôle that is not yours
   Do you strive to act, with a lonely pain?
Forget the grief that your heart endures ;
   Begin once more to be glad again."

But nothing my Bird hath answered me ;
   Only again and again hath tried
The sweet, sad song or the song of glee —
   The strain of the singer, her mate, that died.

UNTOLD.

A FACE may be woeful-white to cover a heart that's
    aching;
And a face may be full of light over a heart that's
    breaking!

'T is not the heaviest grief for which we wear the willow;
The tears bring slow relief which only wet the pillow.

Hard may be burdens borne, though friends would fain
    unbind them;
Harder are crosses worn where none save Christ can
    find them.

For the loved who leave our side our souls are well-nigh
    riven;
But ah! for the graves we hide, have pity, tender
    Heaven!

Soft be the words and sweet that soothe the spoken
    sorrow;
Alas! for the weary feet that may not rest to-morrow.

TRUST FOR THE DAY.

BECAUSE in a day of my days to come
    There waiteth a grief to be,
Shall my heart grow faint, and my lips be dumb,
    In this day that is bright for me?

Because of a subtle sense of pain,
    Like a pulse-beat, threaded through
The bliss of my thought, shall I dare refrain
    From delight in the pure and true?

In the harvest-field shall I cease to glean,
    Since the bloom of the Spring has fled?
Shall I veil mine eyes to the noonday sheen,
    Since the dew of the morn hath sped?

Nay, phantom ill with the warning hand,
   Nay, ghosts of the weary past, —
Serene, as in armor of faith, I stand ;
   Ye may not hold me fast.

Your shadows across my sun may fall,
   But as bright the sun shall shine ;
For I walk in a light ye cannot pall,
   The light of the King divine.

And whatever He sends from day to day,
   I am sure that His name is Love ;
And He never will let me lose my way
   To my rest in His home above.

THE WELCOME.

ANITHER bairn cam' hame —
    Hame to mither and me !
It was yestreen in the gloamin' —
    When scarce was light to see
The wee bit face o' the darlin' —
    That its greetin' cry was heard,
And crowdin' close we made a place
    To haud anither bird !

Sax little bonnie mouths,
    Ah me ! tak' muckle to fill,
But to grudge the bit t' the seventh
    For mither and me were ill !
Oh ! nestle up closer, dearie,
    Lie saft on the snawy breast,
Where fast life's fountain floweth,
    When thy twa warm lips are prest.

The rich man counteth his cares
   By the shinin' gowd in 's hand,
By 's ships that sail on the sea,
   By 's harvests that whiten the land.
The puir man counteth his blessings
   By the ring o' voices sweet,
By the hope that glints in bairnies' een,
   By the sound o' bairnies' feet.

An' it 's welcome hame, my darlin' !
   Hame to mither an' me !
An' it 's never may ye find less o' love
   Than the love ye brought wi' ye !
Cauld are the blasts o' the wild wind,
   An' rough the warld may be,
But warm 's the hame o' the wee one
   In the hearts o' mither an' me !

DINNA CHIDE.

AH ! dinna chide the mither !
   Ye may na hae her lang ;
Her voice, abune your baby rest,
   Sae saftly crooned the sang ;
She thocht ye ne'er a burden,
   She greeted ye wi' joy,
An' heart an' hand in carin' ye,
   Foun' still their dear employ.

Her han' has lost its cunnin',
   It 's tremblin' now and slow,
But her heart is leal an' lovin',
   As it was lang ago !
An' though her strength may wither,
   An' faint her pulses beat,
Nane will be like the mither,
   Sae steadfast, true, an' sweet !

Ye maun revere the mither,
   Feeble an' auld an' gray ;
The shinin' ones are helpin' her
   Adoon her evenin' way !
Her bairns wha wait her yonder,
   Her gude mon gone before :
She wearies — can ye wonder ? —
   To win to that braw shore !

Ah ! dinna chide the mither !
   O lip, be slow to say
A word to vex the gentle heart
   Wha watched your childhood's day ;
Ay, rin to heed the tender voice
   Wha crooned the cradle sang,
An' dinna chide the mither, sin'
   Ye may na hae her lang !

AT THE OLD FARM.

YES, 't is true. The blinds are closed, and the front
    door streams with crape.
Surely through the house last eve stole a vague and awful
    shape,
Dimly seen by only one — viewless, soundless, to the rest :
Only one descried the arrow ere its death-pang pierced
    his breast.

Why, they say he kissed his wife ! She was sitting by the
    door,
With her patient, work-worn hands folded, for the day
    was o'er ;
And the twilight wind stirred softly, tapped the lilacs on
    the pane,
While belated bees swung slowly homeward through the
    scented lane.

" Ruth," he said, and touched her brow, gently as a lover
    might, —
Stooped and kissed her, sitting there.   She was struck
    with sudden fright.
" Ah ! what is it, John?" she cried; " do you think I 'm
    going to die? "
" No !" he answered, "no, dear wife. If 't is any one,
    't is I."

Full ten years or more had passed since he 'd given her
    a word
Thoughtful, feeling-like, caressing. She could scarce be-
    lieve she heard
Rightly now. Their talk, you see, was, most part, about
    the farm —
Butter, eggs, the new Alderney, making hay; they meant
    no harm.

Kindly, honest, Christian folk, both the deacon and his
    wife ;
Only somehow they had lost all the romance out of life.
And the love which they began with, like a flower o'er-
    grown with weeds,
Struggled on, half-choked, half-buried, in the strife for
    worldly needs.

Well, the night came on apace.   All the usual chores
  were done,
And they went to bed as usual; rising always with the
  sun,
'T was not worth while burning candles; and at midnight,
  lo ! a call
Woke the sleepers.   One was taken, one was left — and
  that was all.

Lucy told me of the kiss.   On her way to meet the choir
She had stopped to see Aunt Ruth, — she and Neighbor
  Brown's Desire.
They were not surprised, this morning, when they heard
  that he was dead;
That he must have had a warning was what our Lucy said.

But I think the real love, the true love, — that never dies,
Once two loyal hearts have known it, — wakened 'neath
  those evening skies;
And 't will be a comfort sweet, in her lonely time to be,
That, before he went, he spoke to the " dear wife "
  tenderly.

KNIGHT AND LADY.

HE lifted his hand to his plumed chapeau,
　　He bowed to her beauty and rode away, —
He through the glorious world to go,
　She in the lone little home to stay.

Swift as a vision he passed the fields
　Where the wild rose blushed amid golden grain ;
She took up the weapons which woman wields
　When fain from herself she would hide her pain.

Out in the thickest of noble strife
　He felt the rapture of conflict brave ;
And she, shut into her quiet life,
　Half deemed its narrowness like the grave.

Yet, strange to say, when the war was past,
　And the knight came back wearing valor's stars,
'T was the lady who, wan and pale, at last
　Gave token of wounds which had left their scars.

D O N.

BLACK as a crow, with a satin sheen
    On his well-brushed coat, — with plenty to eat,
Oats and corn and, along between,
The daintiest pasture, rich and sweet, —
In his old age Don leads an easy life,
Though he spent his youth in the thick of the strife.
Now, watch him while the procession comes :
Ah, yes, good fellow, you hear the drums,
Bugles, and trumpets ; you 're brave to-day ;
Head up, ears pricked, you are back in the fray.
    He carried his master at Gettysburg.

Poor Tom ! I 've his diary here on the shelf, —
My dearest treasure, a bit of himself, —
Pencilled at night by the bivouac,
Pencilled in saddle on Don's broad back,
Some of it scrawled in the hospital,
Some inside of the prison's wall.

It tells of pain and hunger and thirst, —
Terse and brief when it tells of the worst,
Jolly and bright with a boy's delight
When the boys are safe over march and fight.
Scraps of Latin are here and there,
And once a tress of bonny brown hair.
There 's never the breath of a weak complaint,
Nor the sign of a word that would vex a saint,
For Tom was bold and tender and true !
I tell you, lady, his mother knew :
From the cradle onward, Tom, my son,
Was a lad you could pin your faith upon.

Did I hear the cannon?   Ay, far and away,
As I sat at my sewing, its dull, faint boom,
Ever and often, that weary day,
Over miles of clover, came straight to my room.
At times I would drop my seam, and pray,
For a shudder crept o'er me again and again ;
But I was as calm as a statue when
I learned, at last, the terrible price
I had paid for my country.   Cold as ice
I waited to see my dear, dead son ;
'T was a comfort that father brought home poor Don.

Do you wonder I 've taken care of him
All these years, till his eye is dim,
And his fire has fled, and his vigor wanes?
Tho' naught but the memory remains
Of the steed he was, yet a sudden flash
Will waken the thrill of the cavalry dash, —
As now, when grand with bugles and drums
Gaily the holiday regiment comes !
Ah ! Don, good Don, you *may* eat your fill,
And browse in the meadow lot at will,
For Tom is asleep, just over the hill,
　　The master you carried at Gettysburg.

ASHES OF ROSES.

FRIEND, in whose eyes I looked to-day,
　　Whose hand in clinging clasp held mine,
The tender word I could not say
　　That from my heart went forth to thine.

So lately all thy life was fair,
　　And bathed in morning's loveliest glow ;
So lately came the frosty air
　　That laid its choicest blossoms low.

Alone by depth of mother-love,
　　I measure depth of mother-loss,
And feel how thick the clouds above
　　Thy weary pathway of the cross.

Yet sorrow reigns a queen on earth.
　　At many a door, a guest unbid,
She lifts the latch ; nor less the hearth
　　She darkens when her form is hid

From stranger eyes, when asphodels
　　Spring, spear-like, by no new-made grave,
Nor gloom of mourning-garment tells
　　How keen a blow her sword-thrust gave.

With insight clear I comprehend
　　Thy stricken life that dreads the sun,
Thy sleepless nights so slow to end,
　　Thy days that creep in silence on.

Still, whether fade the rose of love
　　Before a blighting wind of fate,
Or, angel-borne to realms above,
　　It bloom anew at heaven's gate, —

If once its fragrance blessed our life,
　　We never wholly lose the past ;
Its ashes are with sweetness rife,
　　And make us richer to the last.

And pain hath gems that purely shine,
　　" Through suffering perfect," graven where
They catch the light from Love Divine :
　　Shall we complain, such gems who bear ?

IN GALILEE.

THE Master walked in Galilee,
    Across the hills and by the sea,
And in whatever place he trod,
He felt the passion of a God.

The twelve, who deemed him King of men,
Longed for the conquering hour, when
The peasant's robe without a seam
Should be the purple of their dream.

Yet daily from his lips of love
Fell words their thoughts as far above
As wisdom's utmost treasure, piled
Upon the stammering of a child.

Like frost on flower, like blight on bloom,
His speech to them of cross and tomb;
Nor could their grieving spirits see
One gleam of hope in Galilee.

What booted it that he should rise,
Were death to hide him from their eyes?
What meant the promised throne divine,
Were earth to be an empty shrine?

Low drooped the skies above the band
Too dull the Lord to understand.
Alas! as slow of heart are we,
Abiding oft in Galilee.

MY PRIMROSE.

MY little primrose, gentle flower,
The darling of how many an hour
When thou and I together gaze
In sheltered peace on stormful days.

Above thee broods a quiet hush ;
And yet the shadow of a blush,
That once hath stirred the vestal air,
Is tranced upon thy petals fair.

Nor bird, nor butterfly, nor bee,
Hath ever whispered love to thee,
Nor sunbeam ventured to caress,
Too bold, thy sweet unconsciousness.

Why, then, the dream of roseate glow,
So faint upon thy virgin snow?
Canst thou divine how dear thou art,
White winter blossom, to my heart?

How in thy dainty grace I see
A pledge of lovely things to be,
And wait, when thou hast had thy day,
To greet the flowery fields of May?

The wildwood treasures, coy and sweet,
The bloom of gardens, and the fleet,
Large rapture of the orchard's foam,
In that delightful time to come,

Will say but this, which thou dost say
So softly to my soul to-day :
" The Lord who keeps his promises
Is near thee ever, near to bless.

" No spoken word his heart forgets,
The hour for leaf and bud he sets ;
Who cares for fragile flower shall be
A strong defence to thine and thee."

Smile on, my little primrose fair,
Shed faintest perfume on the air ;
The winds may rave, the rain may fall,
But we are happy through it all.

OUR OWN.

IF I had known in the morning
How wearily all the day
   The words unkind
   Would trouble my mind
I said when you went away,
I had been more careful, darling,
   Nor given you needless pain ;
      But we vex " our own "
      With look and tone
   We might never take back again.

For though in the quiet evening
   You may give me the kiss of peace,
      Yet well it might be
      That never for me
   The pain of the heart should cease.
How many go forth in the morning
   Who never come home at night ;
      And hearts have broken
      For harsh words spoken,
   That sorrow can ne'er set right.

We have careful thought for the stranger,
And smiles for the sometime guest,
But oft for " our own "
The bitter tone,
Though we love our own the best.
Ah ! lip with the curve impatient ;
Ah ! brow with that look of scorn,
'T were a cruel fate
Were the night too late
To undo the work of morn.

THE EDELWEISS.

FAR up on sternest Alpine crests,
　　Where winds of tempest blow,
They say that, all unfearing, rests
　　A flower upon the snow, —
A tiny flower, pale and sweet,
　　That blooms o'er breath of ice ;
And glad are they, on any day,
　　Who find the Edelweiss.

Ah ! far on heights of sorrows cold,
　　Where tears are dropping slow,
Some hearts have found, and, finding, told
　　How fair a flower may grow.
With petals pale, but perfume rare,
　　It garlands days of ice ;
And blessed are they who, weeping, pray,
　　And find Faith's Edelweiss.

THE MARKET–BELL.

SWEET from his pipe the piper drew
    A sound that ravished all men's ears,
And soared ethereal to the blue
    Wherein the skylark disappears.
The listening throng, or grave or gay,
Were hushed beneath the music's sway.

When sudden, on the silver notes,
    A loud, discordant clamor fell;
A shout arose from eager throats:
    "The market-bell! the market-bell!"
Swift rushed the audience from the place;
The piper piped to empty space.

A bitter story this, — antique,
    And full of cynic irony.
The keen-edged humor of the Greek, —
    Hath it no sting for thee and me?
Or glad, or wise, or sad, or fain,
Dear Nature wooes us not in vain!

Her mystic measures round us roll,
  We sit in silence at her feet;
And, awed and thrilled, we own control
  As potent as, alas! 't is fleet.
For list! for hark! we know it well —
Earth's loud, imperious market bell.

FOLLOW ME.

MASTER and servant, through the storm and sleet
And thickening darkness, toiled with weary feet.

Fierce winds came hurtling from the mountain height,
The pines moaned sadly in the bitter night.

Flickering the lantern shed a fitful glow
On paths unbroken, drifted deep with snow.

Courage and fortitude alike outworn,
The servant faltered, frighted and forlorn.

"Home beckons fair," he sighed, "aye sweet and fair,
But I shall never live to enter there."

Eyes clear as stars, lips sweet as rose in bloom,
The Master bent above him in the gloom.

"Arise !" he said, "we cross an evil land ;
The tempest's wrath is wild on every hand.

" But I before thee go to lead the way,
And I will guide thee to the dawn of day.

"Thou hast but this, to set thy feet where mine
Make prints, step after step, a track for thine.

" O faint of heart, let craven terrors flee.
I am thy Lord ; arise and follow me."

Master Divine, by times the upward way
Lies nearer midnight than the dawn of day.

The chill wind smites, the dark pines murmur low,
Faith's waning tapers shine with fitful glow.

The servant needs thy look of majesty ;
Before its light his trembling fears shall flee.

O bend with lips as sweet as rose in bloom ;
O bend with eyes like stars, and pierce the gloom.

Say royally : " Arise and follow Me ;
Step after step, my feet make prints for thee."

MANNA.

'TWAS in the night the manna fell,
That fed the hosts of Israel,

Enough for each day's fullest store
And largest need — enough, no more.

For wilful waste, for prideful show,
God sent not angels' food below.

Still in our nights of deep distress
The manna falls our hearts to bless.

And, famished, as we cry for bread,
With heavenly food our lives are fed.

And each day's need finds each day's store
Enough.   Dear Lord, what want we more?

THE SADNESS OF SUMMER.

O BEAUTIFUL Summer ! thou bringest again
    The pomp of thy life to the children of men ;
The light, once of Eden, lies fair on thy hills,
The echoes of Paradise sing in thy rills ;
Sweet, sweet are thy winds as they wander and sigh
Through the far tops of pines and the green spears of rye,
And warm on thy meadows lies, fold upon fold,
Thy mantle that glimmers with ruby and gold.

O beautiful Summer ! thy roses are free,
And toss in their bloom like the foam of the sea ;
They are crimson like wine, they are white like the snow,
And the breath of their cups is of censers aglow ;
Thy lilies are pure, and all proudly they stand,
Unchallenged and chaste in the jubilant land.
No charm is less potent, no splendor is gone
From the slow-stealing eve or the swift-waking dawn.

So, Summer the royal, the fault is not thine
If thou bear to our spirits more shadow than shine, —

If, grasping thy roses with olden desire,
Too soon of their passionate fragrance we tire ;
In all the rich chords of thy manifold strain,
If to us be a minor, keen-edged as with pain,
Thou bringest back Eden, — an angel of strife
Still bars from our taking its green tree of life.

We are losing the strength of the days that were young,
Our hopes are no longer like banners outflung ;
We have parted with friends who were leal at our side,
The voices of children in silence have died.
Of the plans which we planned, of the works which we
        wrought,
Of the turreted castles of glorious thought,
How little remains ! they are crumbling to dust,
The robes are moth-eaten, the weapons are rust.

And all in rebellion we turn from the good
Thou offerest now.   In perverseness of mood
We cry to thee : " Come not with smile nor with gift,
The cloud of our darkness thy beam shall not rift ;
Laugh on with thy lilies, and garland the hours
With infinite tinting of exquisite flowers ;
Sweet, sweet let thy winds in their gladness go by,
For us there is naught but to sorrow and die."

O beautiful Summer ! we flout thee in vain ;
There is patience with thee, though we, thankless,
    complain.
Thy heart is the mother's.   The mother knows best
When to let the grieved child just lie close to her breast,
With soft arms to clasp it, with kisses to cheer,
With a calm word to soothe it : " My love and my dear,
Wait only,—the trouble will pass with the day."
We hear the sweet whisper, we 're fain to obey.

WILD WEATHER OUTSIDE.

WILD weather outside where the brave ships go,
   And fierce from all quarters the four winds blow —
Wild weather and cold, and the great waves swell,
With chasms beneath them as black as hell.
The waters frolic in Titan play,
They dash the decks with an icy spray,
The spent sails shiver, the lithe masts reel,
And the sheeted ropes are as smooth as steel.
And oh, that the sailor were safe once more
Where the sweet wife smiles in the cottage door!

The little cottage, it shines afar,
O'er the lurid seas, like the polar star.
The mariner tossed in the jaws of death
Hurls at the storm a defiant breath;
Shouts to his mates through the writhing foam,
" Courage ! please God, we shall yet win home ! "
Frozen and haggard and wan and gray,
But resolute still, — 't is the sailor's way;
And perhaps — at the fancy the stern eyes dim —
Somebody 's praying to-night for him.

Ah me, through the drench of the bitter rain,
How bright the picture that rises plain !
Sure he can see, with her merry look,
His little maid crooning her spelling-book ;
The baby crows from the cradle fair ;
The grandam nods in her easy-chair :
While hither and yon, with a quiet grace,
A woman flits, with an earnest face.
The kitten purrs and the kettle sings,
And a nameless comfort the picture brings.

Rough weather outside, but the winds of balm
Forever float o'er that isle of calm.
O friends who read, over tea and toast,
Of the wild night's work on the storm-swept coast, —
Think, when the vessels are overdue,
Of the perilous voyage, the baffled crew,
Of stout hearts battling for love and home
'Mid the cruel blasts and the curdling foam,
And breathe a prayer, from your happy lips,
For those who must go " to the sea in ships ; "
Ask that the sailor may stand once more
Where the sweet wife smiles in the cottage door.

THE PATCHWORK QUILT.

IN sheen of silken splendor,
    With glinting threads of gold,
I 've seen the priceless marvels
    Once hung in halls of old,
Where fair hands wrought the lily,
    And brave hands held the lance,
And stately lords and ladies
    Stepped through the courtly dance.

I 've looked on rarer fabrics,
    The wonders of the loom,
That caught the flowers of summer,
    And captive held their bloom;
But not their wreathing beauty,
    Though fit for queens to wear,
Can with one household treasure,
    That 's all my own, compare.

It has no golden value,
   The simple patchwork spread, —
Its squares in homely fashion
   Set in with green and red ;
But in those faded pieces
   For me are shining bright,
Ah ! many a summer morning,
   And many a winter night.

The dewy breath of clover,
   The leaping light of flame,
Like spells my heart come over,
   As one by one I name
These bits of old-time dresses —
   Chintz, cambric, calico —
That looked so fresh and dainty
   On my darlings long ago.

This violet was mother's ;
   I seem to see her face,
That ever like a sunrise
   Lit up the shadiest place.
This buff belonged to Susan ;
   That scarlet spot was mine ;
And Fannie wore this pearly white,
   Where purple pansies shine.

I turn my patchwork over —
    A book with pictured leaves —
And I feel the lilac fragrance,
    And the snow-fall on the eaves.
Of all my heart's possessions,
    I think it least could spare
The quilt we children pieced at home
    When mother dear was there.

THE BUILDING OF THE NEST.

THEY 'LL come again to the apple-tree —
  Robin and all the rest —
When the orchard branches are fair to see,
  In the snow of the blossom drest;
And the prettiest thing in the world will be
  The building of the nest.

Weaving it well, so round and trim,
  Hollowing it with care, —
Nothing too far away for him,
  Nothing for her too fair, —
Hanging it safe on the topmost limb,
  Their castle in the air.

Ah! mother-bird, you 'll have weary days
  When the eggs are under your breast,
And shadow may darken the dancing rays
  When the wee ones leave the nest;
But they 'll find their wings in a glad amaze,
  And God will see to the rest.

So come to the trees with all your train
   When the apple blossoms blow ;
Through the April shimmer of sun and rain,
   Go flying to and fro ;
And sing to our hearts as we watch again
   Your fairy building grow.

HARVEST.

SPRING hath the morning gladness,
　　The hope of budding leaves ;
And Summer in her queenly lap
　　The wealth of noon receives ;
But Autumn hath the twilight's crown,
　　The joy of garnered sheaves.

Where late in stately phalanx
　　The ribboned corn was seen,
Where the golden wheat was waving,
　　And the oats in silver sheen,
And where the buckwheat snow was white,
　　Hath the reaper's sickle been.

In clouds the purple aster
　　Enfolds the hillsides bare ;
The sumach lifts its vivid plumes
　　Like flame ; the misty air
Hath hints of rainbow splendors
　　Estray and captive there.

The hidden seed that slumbered
　So safe beneath the snow,
With thrills of life was quickened,
　And could not help but grow,
When pierced the sun's entreaties
　The frozen mould below.

By tender love-caressing,
　By silent drops of dew,
Mid sudden storms of passion
　And heats of wrath it grew,
Till the fields were ripe to harvest,
　And the year's long work was through.

The mother-earth is tired —
　No child on mother-breast
Lies soft till after birth-throes ;
　Toil giveth right to rest ;
And all the joy of harvest
　With the peace of God is blest.

APPLE BLOSSOMS.

ALL day in the green, sunny orchard,
 When May was a marvel of bloom,
I followed the busy bee-lovers
 Down paths that were sweet with perfume.

The one perfect cluster I sought for
 Was not in the orchard for me ;
It swung on the edge of a forest,
 From the bough of a wild apple-tree —

A tree that no thrift of the farmer
 Had cared in its life to protect,
All twisted and stunted and barren,
 The orphan of nature's neglect.

That, lone in the lavish Spring beauty,
     Bore only one blossoming spray, —
But that, in its delicate tinting,
     The blossom I 'd looked for all day !

The soul of the tree in its prison
     Had thrilled to the passion of Spring,
And given itself in its answer —
     The beggar-maid's " Yes " to the king.

So told me the gray-bearded painter,
     And showed me the branch that he broke,
All glowing and sweet on the canvas
     The while that he dreamily spoke.

"ELIZABETH, AGED NINE."

OUT of the way in a corner
    Of our dear old attic room,
Where bunches of herbs from the hillside
    Shake ever a faint perfume,
An oaken chest is standing —
    With hasp and padlock and key —
Strong as the hands that made it
    On the other side of the sea.

When the winter days are dreary,
    And we're out of heart with life,
Of its crowding cares are weary
    And sick of its restless strife,
We take a lesson in patience
    From the attic corner dim,
Where the chest holds fast its treasure,
    A warder dark and grim :

Robes of an antique fashion —
   Linen and lace and silk —
That time has tinted with saffron,
   Though once they were white as milk ;
Wonderful baby garments,
   Broidered, with loving care,
By fingers that felt the pleasure
   As they wrought the ruffles rare.

A sword, with the red rust on it,
   That flashed in the battle-tide,
When, from Lexington to Concord,
   Sorely men's hearts were tried ;
A plumed chapeau and a buckle,
   And many a relic fine ;
And all by itself the sampler,
   Framed in by berry and vine.

Faded the square of canvas,
   Dim is the silken thread —
But I think of white hands dimpled,
   And a childish, sunny head ;
For here in cross and tent stitch,
   In a wreath of berry and vine,
She worked it a hundred years ago,
   " Elizabeth, aged nine."

In and out in the sunshine
    The little needle flashed,
And out and in on the rainy day
    When the sullen drops down plashed,
As close she sat by her mother —
    The little Puritan maid —
And did her piece on the sampler
    Each morn before she played.

You are safe in the crystal heavens,
    " Elizabeth, aged nine,"
But before you went you had troubles
    Sharper than any of mine.
The gold-brown hair with sorrow
    Grew white as drifted snow,
And your tears fell here, slow-staining
    This very plumed chapeau.

When you put it away, its wearer
    Would need it never more, —
By a sword-thrust learning the secrets
    God keeps on yonder shore.
But you wore your grief like glory;
    Not yours to yield supine,
Who wrought in your patient childhood,
    " Elizabeth, aged nine."

Out of the way in a corner,
   With hasp and padlock and key,
Stands the oaken chest of my fathers
   That came from over the sea.
The hillside herbs above it
   Shake odors faint and fine,
And here on its lid is a garland
   To " Elizabeth, aged nine."

For love is of the immortal,
   And patience is sublime,
And trouble 's a thing of every day,
   That toucheth every time ;
And childhood sweet and sunny,
   Or womanly truth and grace,
In the dusk of the way light torches,
   And cheer earth's lowliest place.

ERIC'S FUNERAL.

TIRED? Yes, a little, I believe. I'm not so very
    strong,
And older than I was, my dear: I'm sure it won't be
    long
Before *my* turn comes. Life is sweet, but *surely* sweeter
    far,
Where we shall find our faded youth, beyond the morning-
    star.

I've been to Eric's funeral — my old friend Eric Gray.
To think that he is gone! Ah, well! how peaceful-like
    to-day
He looked, as there he lay at rest in narrow coffined
    space,
The snow-white lilies on his breast, the death-white on
    his face!

I mind him years and years ago. A half-remembered
    dream,
A feather-flake of falling snow that melts upon a stream,
To me has yesterday become. My memory fails with
    age,
But all that filled my early home is like a pictured page.

I saw him first at father's house. They held the meeting
    there
On Wednesday evenings, and the church convened for
    praise and prayer ;
The old and young together sat, and lifted up the psalm
In tones that seemed the phrase to fit, with blending
    cadence calm.

Not men of many words were they, grave-browed and
    stern and strong ;
Yet on Predestination they would argue loud and
    long, —
With keenest blades of logic, and with hammer blows of
    will,
The while the women listened there in acquiescence
    still.

" Society " was what they called the Presbyterian band
Of earnest-hearted folk who tried to keep the Lord's
　　command, —
Though hard as iron it might press, and blight their lives
　　with pain, —
Who took earth's joy with thankfulness, and patient bore
　　its bane.

Once more I see, through years of gloom, the candles
　　burning bright,
The row of chairs around the room, the table covered
　　white,
The Bible opened at " the place," and father waiting
　　there,
A light upon his reverent face, and on his silver hair.

By ones and twos the people came, till all the chairs were
　　filled ;
Then one upon the Holy Name would call, and, as God
　　willed,
Would bid Him deal with this His flock, yet haply in
　　His love,
Would dare entreat Him smite the rock, and feed them
　　from above.

" The Lord 's my Shepherd, I 'll not want ; He makes me
    down to lie
In pastures green ; He leadeth me the quiet waters by : "
The sweet old words, the sweet old tune, they bore our
    spirits higher
Than all the tortured music of the cultured modern choir.

It was the psalm their lips had learned beside the mother's
    knee,
Where Scotia's purple heather burned, or dashed the
    Northern Sea.
Oh, loud and clear the anthem rolled ; I often hear it
    still,
As, rippling down from streets of gold, its echoes near me
    thrill.

Slow waned the sacred hour. At last the closing words
    were said ;
Then swift the sparkling moments passed, slipped off a
    silver thread
Of laughter, innocent and low, while youths and maidens
    met,
And lingered, talking, loath to go, like youths and maidens
    yet.

You see yourself in yonder glass?   Well, I was once like
    you,
As softly flushed, as dimple-sweet, when all my life was
    new.
My mother made me braid my hair and keep it smooth
    and plain ;
She feared that curls would be a snare; she would not
    have me vain.

And often as my brothers told what this or that one
    said
Of compliment or courtesy, lest it should turn my
    head,
She gave a flavor of reproof — a dash of bitter-sweet —
To such light words; for beauty's bloom the immortal soul
    might cheat.

There was but one who never seemed to see that I was
    fair,
That in my eyes the sunlight dreamed, and danced upon
    my hair ;
And that was Eric.   So I set my heart on Eric Gray —
For ever what we may not have, that most we prize
    alway.

I showed it not by look or sign — that would have been a
    shame —
But in my heart I made his shrine, and softly named his
    name
In whispers only God could hear, where, kneeling by my
    bed
At night and morning, God was near, and heard the
    prayers I said.

" Let none despise thy youth," was bid to Timothy of old.
None could despise young Eric's truth, his bearing frank
    and bold.
Among his fellows there he stood, in stature lifted high,
Like some straight pine-tree of the wood that towers to
    the sky.

The elders listened when he spoke, the minister took
    heed
(And in those days the minister was some one grand
    indeed).
I thrilled with pride to hear his praise, and still perversely
    tried
To blame him for his rigid ways, and have my blame
    denied.

The sunlight wooes the forest leaf, the moonlight wooes
    the sea,
So by attraction's subtle grace was Eric drawn to me ;
But all the more I loved him, I was iced in maiden
    pride,
And shy and cold and silent whene'er he sought my
    side, —

Till came at last my radiant hour of triumph and delight :
" He loved me." By that gracious dower the world for
    me grew bright ;
My heart was like a cradled nest, where through enchanted
    days
There lived a sweet-voiced singing-guest that sang his
    love always.

" What parted us ? " For Eric Gray had wife and chil-
    dren dear,
And I, in Scottish phrase, " have lived my lane " this
    many a year.
A widowed wife will wear for him the widow's shrouding
    veil,
Though she was never first whose robes in densest woe
    will trail.

"Who is that happy girl?" they said, who saw me at that
    time,
When common days went trippingly, like tuneful words
    that rhyme.
But Eric's mother did not smile. She thought that levity
Ill suited one whom he, " my son," had chosen his bride
    to be.

So when, for very rapture, in the glory of my life, —
The color and the perfume, of which its bloom was
    rife, —
I let my gladness overflow, and acted like the child
I was, she talked to Eric with warning accents mild,

And bade me read the Proverbs, where the prudent wife
    is praised.
I listened, little pleased ; and more — I felt incensed,
    amazed.
My dear, if you would like to make a sinner of a saint,
Just take her to the Bible, with an air of vexed complaint.

I had not joined the church. I knew within me, sweet
    and clear,
A tenderness, as if that One Divinely Good were near ;

I loved that Presence, but my heart accepted not the
    creed
That made me willing to be lost, if thus the Lord had
    need.

The gentle words that Jesus spoke were bread of life to
    me ;
But, overlaid with doctrines fierce of duty and decree,
I could not say I took them all, as father thought I
    should,
And as at worship, night and morn, he often prayed I
    would.

Eric, he often talked to me, and urged me, still in vain,
To go before the elders and to let them make it plain ;
And so our lovers' interviews grew into hot debate
Upon Electing Love, and Faith, and Mankind's Lost Estate.

At last one day, with mournful face, he said, " It is a sin
To marry, if not in the Lord.   All glorious within
Should be the daughter of the King."   I, smiling, set him
    free.
Heart's love, true love, *is* in the Lord ; but that he did
    not see.

He married Jennie MacIntyre. She 'd tried to win him
  long.
They say his life has not been quite as merry as a
  song.
He gathered wealth of lands and gold, his vessels crossed
  the sea,
But his stately home was grim and cold, as what else
  could it be

With her?   " You 're sorry for my life "?   Nay, darling,
  all is best :
I 'm surer of it as my sun leans down the golden west.
I was too quick and passionate, perhaps, for Eric Gray,
And I have lived in God's content, safe-folded, all my
  way.

But there at Eric's funeral, the lilies on his breast,
The lilies and the sheaf of wheat, and the aged face at
  rest,
With something of the look it wore, the young look back
  again —
It brought the old days here once more, the pleasure and
  the pain.

And all my heart went forward, past the shadow and the
    cross,
Even to that home where perfect love hath never thorn nor
    loss ;
Where neither do they marry, nor in marriage are they
    given,
But are like unto the angels in God's house, which is
    Heaven.

CHRYSANTHEMUMS.

WHEN the last red leaves are shining in the rich
    October sun,
When the twilight, early falling, melts in dreamy dusk
    away,
Ere the sweet cicada's chirping in the aftermath is done,
    Comes my favorite flower of autumn, to illume the
    pensive day.

Pensive, though in stately splendor, sits the Year, her
    toiling o'er, —
    Pensive still, though on her forehead gleam the jewels
    of a queen ;
For her roses and her lilies bloom around her feet no
    more,
    And her waving fields have bent them to the sickle
    bright and keen.

With a fragrance aromatic, with a wild and careless grace,
　As if somehow to the garden came the freedom of the
　　woods,
Lifts each fair chrysanthemum her dear, captivating face,
　Filled with sympathy for us, in our fluctuating moods.

White as bridal robe of beauty, flushed with crimson,
　　blushing deep,
　Flaming high with gold, which, torch-like, flings a glory
　　on the air, —
Through all changes, seems this flower vestal purity to
　keep,
　And its breath hath less of passion than of soft,
　　entreating prayer.

Most, I deem, like woman's courage, strongest when the
　　skies are drear,
　Is this fearless loveliness, lighting bravely all the way,
Through the autumn weeks, till winter with its storms
　　shall close the year,
　And the fury of the tempest whirl athwart the darken-
　　ing day.

BITTER–SWEET.

WHENCE that fragrant name of thine,
    Spicy as the beaded wine?
In what cup of fairy mould,
First were poured thy berries cold,
And what dainty revellers meet
Round thy clusters, Bitter-sweet?

Haply in the deep greenwood
Hebe near thee sponsor stood;
Venus cast thy perfect shape
Tinier than the mountain grape;
And such gods as Homer knew
Gathered thee in dusk and dew.

Lovely birth of frost and fire,
Satisfying all desire;
Though the aster blooms no more,
And the gentian's smile is o'er,
They who rest and they who toil
Count thee Nature's richest spoil.

Life itself is bitter-sweet,
In its rhythm most complete.
Through its loftiest choral strain
Steals the undertone of pain,
And its sober autumn days
Often wake profoundest praise.

Therefore, when the loosened leaf,
Robed in glory bright and brief,
Silent through the crystal air
Floats ethereal as a prayer,
It is joy thy blush to meet,
Jewel-gleaming Bitter-sweet.

For so plain we hear thee say,
" Love is in the world to stay,
Though the seasons wax and wane,
Though the winter come again,"
That our faltering hearts grow strong,
And our lips uplift a song.

A SUMMER MORNING.

ONE set apart in days of old
    From crowded haunts and mortal eyes,
Saw gates, like leaves of pearl unfold,
    And heard the harps of Paradise,
While o'er his thoughts, a hallowed spell,
The present sense of heaven, fell.

So, shimmering through the mountain mist
    I, too, a miracle behold :
A temple, brave with amethyst,
    And opal tints and gleams of gold,
In mystic beauty deigns to rear
Its pomps of pillared splendor here.

Fair house of God, not made with hands,
    Thy walls are laid beneath the sea ;
Thy glittering arches span the lands
    In light aerial symmetry ;
Thy dome is crowned with living fire,
Thou long enchantment of desire.

And far along thy sweeping nave
  Are fragrant censers swinging low ;
And sweet from solemn architrave
  The blending echoes meet and flow —
As bird and flower, awakening, pour
Their rapture through thine open door.

O silver dawn ! O listening hush !
  O kindling glory of the morn !
What beauty in the roseate flush,
  What sheen of gems on leaf and thorn !
How near to God the spirit waits
Who worships in the morning gates.

PASTURE LANDS.

"GREEN pastures," said the Psalmist,
   In that old strain of praise
Which pours its matchless music o'er
   Our rough and rugged ways;
Which rests us with its tenderness,
   As when a mother sings,
And to our weary moods of pain
   Divinest healing brings.

"Green pastures." Pent in city walls
   I think of them to-day, —
How cool and sunny sweet they stretch
   O'er uplands far away;
How velvet-soft their hill-slopes lie,
   How long their shadows sweep,
How tranquil are their silences,
   Their evening peace how deep!

O quiet miles on miles of green !
   O fields with clover fair !
Where flocks repose, where happy birds
   Salute the morning air ;
Where never alien step intrudes,
   Nor harsh invader comes,
Nor peals the great world's bugle blast,
   Nor beats its martial drums.

Had I the wings of eagle strong,
   Or of the gentle dove,
How would I seek your solitudes,
   Your calm, embracing love !
And yet, where hearts in fellowship
   Around me closely stand,
Where loyal hands are clasping mine,
   Must be my pasture-land.

And He who clothes the meadows,
   And weaves the radiant light
Of flower and vine, on mountain sides,
   And through the valleys bright,
Shall give to me the pasture green,
   The waters still and sweet,
Oft as I take my need, my thirst,
   And bend me at His feet.

BEFORE THE FROST.

THERE 's a little pause of waiting, in the time that
    falls between
Nature's waking and her sleeping, ere the white hath hid
    the green,
Which of all the glad year's gladness hath the most of
    rare and fine,
Which of all the sad year's sadness pours elixir most
    divine.

For so blend our lights and shadows, like the crossing
    warp and woof,
That our bliss is edged with sorrow, and full oft our joy is
    proof
Only of some pain that, passing, leaves our spirit's life
    possessed
Of a sense of tranquil pleasure or the dear delight of rest.

In these days of quiet beauty, when the silver haze of
    morn
Like a mystic veil uplifteth and afar to space is borne,
Come the hours like radiant angels bringing gifts from
    One we love,
And the rapture of thanksgiving rises to His throne
    above.

Yet the tears o'erbrim the eyelids as we look from height
    to height,
Flooded with a wondrous splendor, bathed in waves of
    liquid light ;
As we gaze o'er field and forest, where, unrolling rich and
    wide,
Glory still excelleth glory in a vast triumphal tide.

Not the sweet, shy charm of April, not the roseate
    grace of June,
Nor the lilied later summer sleeping in the August noon,
Have such power to stir our longings, have such memo-
    ries dear and deep,
As this time when earth is hushing, like a child before
    its sleep.

Voices once that made our music, fill no more the lonely
    days ;
Faces once that made our sunshine, beam no longer on
    our ways ;
Hands which clasped our own so warmly, folded lie be-
    neath the sod,
And above their strange quiescence, blooms and fades the
    golden rod.

Still our souls go forth undaunted, victors amid loss and
    strife ;
And we gather consolation, in whatever stress of life,
From the thought that over yonder, where the immortal
    anthems swell,
There is utmost peace and safety, and with Christ the
    ransomed dwell.

In the morning-glories' twining, with their fragile trumpet
    shapes,
In the ecstatic thrill of color flushing o'er the ripened
    grapes,
Through the grand year's coronation, beats the loving
    heart of God ;
Let us raise our psalms majestic, let us tell His praise
    abroad !

IN COMMON DAYS.

IN days supreme, of fond delight,
 When happy thoughts within us dwell,
Like vestals robed in stainless white, —
 Who time their footsteps by the swell
Of sweet-voiced bells upon the air —
Then have we least the need for prayer.

In days obscured by veiling folds
 Of grief, or clouded o'er with dread,
While dumb suspense relentless holds
 Its sword above the shrinking head, —
Then, even in the soul's despair,
Is not the deepest need of prayer.

Since to the dark Gethsemane
 The pitying angels, soon or late,
Must come with tenderest ministry,
 And each blithe day is but the gate
To some rich temple, rising fair,
Which builds to heaven a golden stair —

God keep us through the common days,
    The level stretches, white with dust,
When thought is tired, and hands upraise
    Their burdens feebly, since they must.
In days of slowly fretting care,
Then most we need the strength of prayer.

AN EVENING REVERIE.

SINCE climbed the trembling light of dawn far up the
 Eastern stairs,
How long it seems, how very long, since low I knelt at
 prayers,
And strove to cast on Christ the Lord the day with all
 its cares.

Then peace in silver waves came down, and all my soul
 was still ;
The quiet of a deep content my being seemed to fill,
As " Not mine own," I cried, " but Thine be done, Thy
 blessèd will."

I thought : " Whatever He may send to-day, of joy or pain,
So Love decree it, let it come, it cannot come in vain ;
'T will only be a link the more in Love's immortal chain."

I thought : "This day my words shall be so spirit-meek
    and mild,
My steps shall pattern after His, whom never sin defiled,
And I will live in gentleness, because I am His child."

Alas ! with wayside dust assoiled, by wayside thickets
    torn,
With stain of earth upon my robes, and weary and for-
    lorn,
The evening finds me on the day in such calm beauty
    born.

Remembrance folds her mantle o'er a shamed and blush-
    ing face,
And Hope upon the tablet of my heart finds little space
For tracery of golden words, or whispers sweet with
    grace.

How has the evil motive marred the fairest seeming
    deed !
How far the life has been below the lofty - sounding
    creed !
How little has the self been lost to help a brother's
    need !

The thoughtless word, the tone unkind, the shaft by passion sent,
The priceless hour — by angels brought — in idle dreaming spent,
The prison bars that, round the soul, the world and sin
have pent.

For these the bitter tears must fall, as bending low I
pray :
"O Saviour of Thine erring ones, receive this broken
day,
Nor, for my little thought of Thee, take Thou Thy thoughts
away ! "

A WINTER SUNSET.

A WONDERFUL glory of color,
  A splendor of shifting light —
Orange and scarlet and purple —
  Flamed in the sky to-night.
Over the rolling river,
  And over the busy town,
Soft as a benediction
  The rich rays floated down.

They turned the sails of the fishers
  Into opal, rose, and gold ;
The tall and smoky chimneys
  Were like castle turrets bold.
Nothing of plain or common,
  But took a halo strange,
In the light of the lovely sunset,
  With its fairy spell of change.

The day had been long and gloomy,
　Weary with mist and rain,
A day for the heart to brood on
　Sorrow and loss and pain ;
But there came, with the light of evening,
　A wind that swept away
All the shadow and darkness
　Out of the winter day.

Is thy life, O pilgrim, dreary,
　Veiled from the cheery light?
Perhaps for thee is the promise
　Of joy with the waning light.
Fairer than noonday splendor,
　Richer than beams of stars,
The lustrous glory of sunset
　May burn through golden bars.

For ever the sun is shining ;
　If only thy soul can wait,
It will find the light and beauty,
　Though they seem to tarry late.
The soundless, sun-bright portal
　Will suddenly swing apart,
And the grace of the life immortal
　Will guerdon thy trusting heart.

THE TROUBLESOME BABY.

THE little ones cling to the mother,
    With kisses that softly fall,
But somehow the troublesome baby
    Is nearest her heart of all, —
    Ill and fretful and small,
    But dearest to mother of all.

The neighbors wonder and pity,
    Hearing its querulous cry.
" She is losing her youth and beauty,"
    Say friends as they pass her by :
    " Well were the babe to die,
    And the mother have rest," they sigh.

But over the wee white cradle,
    Her soft eyes full of prayer,
Bendeth the weary mother ;
    And never was face so fair,
    Pale, and tired with care, —
    But the glory of love is there !

Rosy and round and dimpled,
  Dewy with childish sleep,
She tucks in her other darlings,
  Whom angels watch and keep.
  Ah, if a darker angel
  Anear this treasure creep !

Bless thee, beautiful mother !
  Thy heart hath a place for all, —
Room for the joys and the sorrows,
  However fast they fall ;
  Room for the baby small,
  That may love thee better than all.

THE FIRST FIRE OF THE SEASON.

HOW it leaps, in dance excited,
How it sleeps, in trance delighted,
How it looms in liquid shining,
How it glooms in wan declining, —
While around the hearth we gather,
One and all,
In the bleak and windy weather
Of the Fall !

Hark ! Without the storm is raging,
Fierce the rout the day engaging ;
Tramp the rains in steady column,
Timed to strains of music solemn, —
But within, the house is cheery ;
There belong
Accents gentle, laughter merry,
Book and song.

Whence art thou, O rare magician,
Weaving now in swift transition
Spells of peaceful incantation
O'er our equal sequestration
  Here at home?   The world behind us,
    Cares forgot,
  Closer while the moments bind us, —
    Blest our lot.

Friendly flame !   Remote Chaldean
Seers of name effaced, Sabean
Shepherds in the elder ages,
Persian bards in mystic pages,
  Thee adored, for so divinely
    Streamed thy light ;
  Half we follow, and enshrine thee,
    Spirit bright !

For thy genial incandescence
Owns no menial-mingled essence ;
Thou wert born of happy seasons,
Child of morn and dew.   The reasons
  Of our love go back to summers
    Long ago,
  And our thoughts, like festive comers,
    Round thee flow.

Dear the friends each heart remembers,
As in cheer we stir the embers,
Bid the ash renew its beauty,
Sparkle, flash, and glow, till duty,
  Through the comfort of the hour,
      Wooes our soul,
  And we deem its sternest dower
      Life's best goal.

So we dream not, visionary,
When we think thee missionary,
Household fire, once more relighted,
Blazing higher, — the while united
  Round the hearth of home we gather,
      One and all,
  In the bleak and windy weather
      Of the Fall.

WHITER THAN SNOW.

WHITER than snow! The soft flakes, shod with peace,
   Dropped silently adown the stirless air,
Till folded under their thick-sheltering fleece
  The brown earth lay, that late was chill and bare.
Can aught be whiter than this whiteness pure?
And yet God's word is true, His promise sure.

O Lord, I lift that vehement prayer of old.
   My sins as scarlet are ; my life, to Thee
An open page, how deeply marred !   Yet bold
   I plead for cleansing.   Jesus' blood shall free
This soul of mine from shame, from guilt, from woe ;
O wash me, Lord, yes, whiter than the snow.

Then, let my feet be swift to run for Thee,
   My hands essay Thy lowliest work to do,
My heart be warm with love, my gladness be
  To hear Thy voice and know its accents true.
And still, where Thou shalt summon may I go,
O Friend Divine, thrice blessed to serve Thee so.

And mid earth's Winter silence, drifted deep,
    When fond hopes fail, when blossoms sweet decay,
When dear ones leave us, and alone we keep
    Grief's mournful vigils in the darkening day,
Still let our souls be patient.   Summer's glow
Abides where Christ's redeemed ones surely go.

AN AUTUMN DAY.

LIKE a jewel, golden-rimmed ;
    Like a chalice, nectar-brimmed ;
Like a strain of music low,
Lost in some sweet long ago ;
Like a fairy story old,
By the lips of children told ;
Like a rune of ancient bard ;
Like a missal glory-starred, —
Comes upon her winsome way
This enchanting Autumn day.

O'er the hills the sunlight sleeps ;
Through the vales the shadow creeps ;
On the river's stately tides,
Rich the silent splendor glides ;
Where the bowery orchards be,
Perfumed breezes wander free ;

Where the purple clusters shine
Through the network of the vine,
Fragrant odors fill the air ;
Beauty shineth everywhere,
While upon her joyous way
Comes the lovely Autumn day.

By the road's neglected banks
Rise the sumach's serried ranks ;
Ragged hedge of thorn and brier
Sudden flames with living fire ;
From the hard unlovely sod
Springs the glancing golden-rod ;
Light the level sunbeams sift
Through the violet aster-drift ;
All her spears in proud array,
Comes the bannered Autumn day.

Lifts the forest's lofty line,
Sceptred oak and solemn pine ;
Shifting rainbow tints illume
All the depths of fronded gloom ;
Through the vista'd aisles unroll
Sweeping robe and trailing stole, —
Where superbly on her way
Comes the royal Autumn day.

Heart of mine, be glad and gay;
Wear thy festival array;
Sing thy song for gathered fruit;
Why shouldst thou alone be mute,
When the winds, from sea to sea,
Ring in chords of jubilee?
After waiting, after prayer,
After pain and toil and care,
After expectation long —
Lo! the bright fulfilments throng.
Gleam the apples through the leaves;
Thickly stand the golden sheaves;
Earth is all in splendor drest;
Queenly fair, she sits at rest,
While the deep delicious day
Dreams its happy life away.

OUR LOST.

THEY never quite leave us, our friends who have passed
    Through the shadows of death to the sunlight
    above ;
A thousand sweet memories are holding them fast
    To the places they blest with their presence and love.

The work which they left and the books which they read
    Speak mutely, though still with an eloquence rare ;
And the songs that they sung, the dear words that they
    said,
    Yet linger and sigh on the desolate air.

And oft when alone, and as oft in the throng,
    Or when evil allures us or sin draweth nigh,
A whisper comes gently, " Nay, do not the wrong,"
    And we feel that our weakness is pitied on high.

We toil at our tasks in the burden and heat
  Of life's passionate noon ; they are folded in peace.
It is well ; we rejoice that their heaven is sweet,
  And one day for us all the bitter will cease.

We, too, shall go home o'er the river of rest,
  As the strong and the lovely before us have gone ;
Our sun will go down in the beautiful west,
  To rise in the glory that circles the throne.

Until then we are bound by our love and our faith
  To the saints who are walking in Paradise fair ;
They have passed beyond sight at the touching of death,
  But they live, like ourselves, in God's infinite care.

GROWING OLD.

IS it parting with the roundness
    Of the smoothly moulded cheek?
Is it losing from the dimples
    Half the flashing joy they speak?
Is it fading of the lustre
    From the wavy golden hair?
Is it finding on the forehead
    Graven lines of thought and care?

Is it dropping — as the rose-leaves
    Drop their sweetness, over-blown —
Household names that once were dearer,
    More familiar than our own?
Is it meeting on the pathway
    Faces strange and glances cold,
While the soul with moan and shiver
    Whispers sadly, " Growing old "?

Is it frowning at the folly
  Of the ardent hopes of youth ?
Is it cynic melancholy,
  At the rarity of truth?
Is it disbelief in loving,
  Selfish hate, or miser's greed?
Then such blight of what was noble
  Is a " growing old " indeed.

But the silver thread that shineth
  Whitely in the thinning tress,
And the pallor where the bloom was,
  Need not tell of bitterness ;
And the brow's more earnest writing,
  Where it once was marble fair,
May be but the spirit's tracing
  Of the peace of answered prayer.

If the smile have gone in deeper,
  And the tear more quickly start,
Both together meet in music
  Low and tender in the heart ;
And in others' joy and gladness
  When the life can find its own,
Surely angels lean to listen
  To the sweetness of the tone.

Nothing lost of all we planted
    In the time of budding leaves,
Only some things bound in bundles
    And set by — our precious sheaves ;
Only treasure kept in safety
    Out of reach, away from rust,
Till the future shall restore it,
    Richer for our present trust.

On the gradual sloping pathway,
    As the passing years decline,
Gleams a golden love-light, falling
    Far from upper heights divine ;
And the shadows from that brightness
    Wrap them softly in their fold,
Who unto celestial whiteness
    Walk, by way of " growing old."

CHRISTMAS–TIDE.

AT Christmas-tide the fields are bare,
   A shiver of frost is in the air;
The wind blows keen across the wold,
Gone is the autumn's glimmer of gold;
But lo ! a red rose opens wide
In the glowing light of the ingleside —
A rose whose fragrance, sweet and far,
Is shed at the beaming of Bethlehem's star;
And once again the angels sing
That Love is heaven and Christ is King.

At Christmas-tide the children go
With dancing footsteps over the snow;
At Christmas-tide the world is bright
With the sudden splendor that thrilled the night,
And made the dawn a shining way,
When first earth wakened to Christmas-day.

Ah ! hide your faces, churls and rude,
For none have a heart to share your mood ;
At Christmas-tide the open hand
Scatters its bounty o'er sea and land.
And none are left to grieve alone,
For Love is heaven and claims its own.

At Christmas-tide there are chiming bells :
Oh, silvery clear their cadence swells.
They smite the cold of Arctic plains,
They ripple through falling of tropic rains ;
In palaces men pause to hear
The wonderful message of peace and cheer ;
In lowly huts the peasants pray
With blessing to God for the happy day.
On every breeze the joy is borne
Around the globe on the Christmas morn ;
And loud once more the angels sing
That Love is heaven and Christ is King.

At Christmas-tide like incense-fires
Arise the chants of stately choirs,
And priestly voices lead the prayers
Where God's dear children cast their cares

Low at the feet of the mighty Lord,
Whose grace is pledged in His deathless word.
And grateful spirits haste to lay
Gifts at his altars on Christmas-day;
While high above the seraphs sing
That Love is heaven and Christ is King.

THE GATE OF PRAYER.

IN a dream I seemed to stand
   By the golden Gate of Prayer,
And to and fro from the shining land,
   Went angels strong and fair.
I heard their beautiful feet,
   I saw their wings sweep by,
And the silver sound of their voices sweet,
   Came thrilling from the sky.

And some as they went were glad,
   A jubilant victor train ;
And some had faces stern and sad, —
   The angels, these, of pain ;
And some came wearily back,
   As if earthly sorrow's pall
Could almost shadow the sunlit track,
   Where the angel footsteps fall.

And I saw that all the host
    Paused just inside the door,
Where the glory of the Holy Ghost
    Lies soft for evermore.
And there was a Face I knew,
    A Face so sad, so sweet ;
And ever the prayers came floating through
    The gate, its look to meet.

Sad was the Face of Christ
    By the golden Gate of Prayer,
Sad for the souls whose weary tryst
    Made mournful murmur there.
Yet its light was clear and still,
    And its smile to my heart was balm,
As over the world, with its seething ill,
    He looked in heavenly calm.

And low to the angel throng :
    " To the happy ones," He said,
" Go forth with ease and strength and song ; "
    (Gayly their errands sped ;)
" But these who seek my face
    With feet that have missed the way,
Myself will bring to a quiet place,
    In the dark and cloudy day."

Oh, not in a dream I kneel
　To-day, by the Gate of Prayer,
Since over my yearning spirit falls
　The quiet that broodeth there ;
And not in a dream I ask :
　" Dear Lord, whatever it be
Of sorrow or pain or daily task
　I bear, come Thou to me."

BESIDE THE BARS.

GRANDMOTHER'S knitting has lost its charm ;
 Unheeded it lies in her ample lap,
While the sunset's crimson, soft and warm,
 Touches the frills of her snowy cap.

She is gazing on two beside the bars,
 Under the maple, — who little care
For the growing dusk, or the rising stars,
 Or the hint of frost in the autumn air.

One is a slender slip of a girl,
 And one a man in the pride of youth, —
The maiden pure as the purest pearl,
 The lover strong in his steadfast truth.

" Sweet, my own, as a rose of June,"
 He says full low, o'er the golden head.
It would sound to her like a dear old tune,
 Could Grandmother hear the soft words said.

For it seems but a little while ago
   Since under the maple, beside the bars,
She stood a girl, while the sunset's glow
   Melted away 'mid the evening stars.

And one, her lover so bright and brave,
   Spake words as tender in tones as low ;
They come to her now from beyond the grave,
   The words of her darling so long ago.

" My own one, sweet as the rose in June ! "
   Her eyes are dim, and her hair is white,
But her heart keeps time to the old love-tune
   As she watches her daughter's child to-night.

A world between them, perhaps you say ;
   Yes — one has read the story through.
One has her beautiful yesterday,
   And one, to-morrow fair to view.

And little you dream how fond a prayer
   Goes up to God, through His silver stars,
From the aged woman gazing there,
   For the two who linger beside the bars.

SUMMER FRUITS.

WHEN scarlet strawberries first were seen
    A blush their clustering leaves between,
I thought that never fruit could be
Delicious as the strawberry.

When cherries ripened firm and fine,
The blackbirds shared their feast with mine,
And Summer's sunshine seemed to glow
On satin skin and heart of snow.

When threaded close on slender stems
The currants gleamed like priceless gems;
When peaches held the velvet cheek
The south wind's coy caress to seek;

The loveliest which I could not choose,
Unwilling one fair gift to lose,
Where frost and fire, and old and new,
And night and day, and dusk and dew,

Had blent to tinge the living sap
And shape the cup for Nature's lap.
Now near and far the apple's wealth
Is servitor of joy and health,

And all along the vineyard's line
The purple grapes are sweet as wine,
For He who pledges daily bread,
With bounty hath our table spread.

And as the singing winds go by,
The drifting odors make reply;
And brook and forest, mount and flood,
Chant " Praise the Lord, for He is good."

VALDEMAR THE HAPPY.

FAVORED in love, and first in war,
Ever had been King Valdemar.

Bards had written heroic lays,
Minstrels had sung in Valdemar's praise.

Mothers had taught their babes his name,
Maidens had dreamed it : this is fame.

Beautiful eyes grew soft and meek
When Valdemar opened his mouth to speak.

Warriors grim obeyed his word,
Nobles were proud to call him Lord.

" Favored in love and famed in war,
Happy must be King Valdemar ! "

So, as he swept along in state,
Muttered the crone at the palace gate, —

Laughing, to clasp in her withered palms
The merry monarch's golden alms.

Home at evening, for rest is sweet,
Tottered the beggar's weary feet.

Home at evening from chase and ring,
Buoyant and brave, came Court and King.

Flickered the lamp in the cottage room,
Flickered the lamp in the castle's gloom.

One went forth at the break of day,
Asking alms on the king's highway.

One lay still at the break of day —
A king uncrowned, a heap of clay.

For swiftly, suddenly, in the night,
A wind of death had put out the light.

And never again might Valdemar,
Strike lance for love or lance for war.

Silent, as if on holy ground,
The weeping courtiers throng around.

Tenderly, as his mother might,
They turn the face to the morning light, —

Loose his garments at throat and wrist,
Softly the silken sash untwist.

Under the linen soft and white,
What surprises their aching sight?

Fretting against the pallid breast,
Find they a penitent's sackcloth vest.

Seamed and furrowed and stained and scarred,
Sadly the flesh of the king is marred.

Never had monk under serge and rope,
Never had priest under alb and cope,

Hidden away with closer art
The passion and pain of a weary heart,

Than had he whose secret torture lay
Openly shown in the light of day.

At the lips all pale and the close-shut eyes,
Long they gazed in their mute surprise —

Eyes once lit with the fire of youth,
Lips that had spoken words of truth.

From each to each there floated a sigh :
" Had this man reason? Then what am I ? "

O friend, think not that stately step,
That lifted brow or that smiling lip,

That sweep of velvet or fall of lace,
Or robes that cling with regal grace,

Are signs that tell of a soul at rest :
Peace seldom hides in a Valdemar's breast.

She shrinks away from the palace glare,
To the peasant's hut and the mountain air,

And kisses the crone at the palace gate,
While the poor, proud king is desolate.

PEACE.

THEY all shall pass : the radiant days
    Song-threaded, flashing quick with light,
And those that, veiled in gloomful haze,
    Creep on, slow-pulsing, to the night.
Upon its outward wave, the last
    Will float us to the tranquil sea,
Where, all the storms forever past,
    Shall peace in tidal fulness be.

There no harassing care shall fret,
    Nor ever vague foreboding chill,
Shall fall no shadow of regret ;
    Shall jar no dissonance of ill, —
Beyond the tumult, fierce and rude,
    Of earthly loss and earthly gain,
Beyond the soul's disquietude,
    Beyond the body's mortal pain.

In all our loneliness we wait,
   In all our weariness we hope ;
The harbor of the Golden Gate
   Before our longing eyes shall ope.
With broken mast and shivered spar,
   We drift adown the darkling sea,
But shines before us like a star,
   O God, our home, our peace in Thee.

IN AN UPPER ROOM.

WITHIN an upper chamber,
    At evening of the day,
We gathered for an hour ;
    And one said, " Let us pray."

We came with stains of conflict,
    With dust of earthly care ;
Our hearts were spent and weary,
    Till Jesus met us there.

We heard no blare of trumpets,
    We saw no blaze of light,
As silently the Master
    Came through the summer night.

Yet was that upper chamber
    With love divinely filled ;
Our hearts grew strong with gladness,
    In that dear presence thrilled.

The air was soft with blessing;
  And as we sang the hymn,
Its notes were lifted higher
  By listening seraphim.

We told our want and yearning,
  We told our lonely pain,
Ere from that upper chamber
  We sought the world again.

But sweet and close and tender,
  In every tranquil breast,
We bore a thought of Jesus —
  Our own, our peace, our rest.

We might have wished to linger
  A little longer there;
But life is full of duty,
  And work is wrought by prayer.

To-day, through strife and turmoil,
  Our eyes shall look above,
Where, in an upper chamber,
  Abides the Lord we love.

MERCHANTMEN.

LONG ago I stood by the sea,
    And sent my ships away from me :

Some with pennons and streamers dight,
Gayly fluttering in the light ;

Some with freight of price untold,
Paid for out of my spirit's gold.

Over the rounding waves afar,
They sailed by sun and sailed by star, —

Over the billows, feather-tipped,
Till out of my sight the last one dipped.

Then I waited and watched and prayed,
The while my absent ships delayed.

One by one, from ports afar,
They sailed by sun and sailed by star ;

Till over the billows, capped with foam,
One by one my ships came home :

Some with the brilliant colors lost,
Some by adverse currents crossed ;

Some with freight of wealth untold,
Worth its weight, from a mine of gold.

But ah ! the ship loved best of all
Never came home to my heart at all.

And often now, as I sit by the sea,
Whereon so many bright hopes be,

I wonder and wonder what befell
The fated ship that I loved so well.

THE NIGHT OUR DARLING DIED.

I 'M thinking of an evening, a weary time ago,
    When the bitter winds of sorrow about our hearth did
      blow, —
When a shadow settled darkly where sunshine erst did
      bide, —
Of the mystery of life and death, the night our darling
      died.

'T was a night in drear November; the spirits of the
      breeze
Were holding rout and revel amid the leafless trees ;
They tapped, with shivering fingers, at our pleasant
      fireside,
But we heeded not their presence the night our darling
      died.

She was but a child, a wee one.   Six happy summers shed
Their meed of golden beauty upon her little head ;
Six years of bliss unclouded in melody did glide,
Ere God sent down the angels the night our darling died.

We watched the fitful brightness, the mournful look of pain,
And hope would light in flashes, or sadly sink again ;
We saw the death-mists gather our star of life to hide,
Yet the fount of tears was frozen, the night our darling
    died.

She moaned a word of sweetness, a little word of love,
And a smile shone for a moment, reflected from above ;
Then the waiting ones enclasped her in their downy
    pinions wide,
And away, away they bore her, our darling and our pride.

There was rustling of bright pinions, there were seraph
    murmurs sweet,
And the shadowed room was holy with the tread of angel-
    feet ;
It had been the gate of heaven to a spirit purified :
But we knew not, and we cared not, the night our dar-
    ling died.

We could only touch the forehead, so ivory-veined and
    chill ;
We could only part the ringlets in childish beauty still ;
We could only fold the white hands on the strangely
    silent breast ;
We could only see the mortal, — the soul had gone to rest.

There are times when two worlds, meeting, clasp with a
    golden band,
And the mourner standeth closest to the radiant Better-
    land :
And, though we thought not of it, bright Heaven was at
    our side
In the hours of weary watching, that night our darling
    died.

TRINITY CHIMES:

ON A SATURDAY AFTERNOON.

THE light of the Indian Summer
   Fell soft on bright Broadway,
Where the ebb and flow of commerce
   Throbbed swift and strong all day ;
And men with anxious thoughts oppressed
   Passed on the crowded way.

In the surging throngs were people
   With weary, care-dimmed eyes,
Who had half-forgotten the story
   Of a heavenly Paradise, —
And, bent with earthly burdens, walked
   Unconscious of the skies :

When clear from the old church steeple
  A message, silver-sweet,
Like a chorus of angel music,
  Thrilled all the busy street;
And " Peace on Earth," the chiming bells
  Seemed softly to repeat.

They chimed the tune of Martyrs,
  And the air of wild Dundee,
And quaint Balerma's measure,
  And Zephyr's harmony;
Then floated o'er that listening throng
  " Nearer, my God, to Thee !"

O folding love of heaven,
  Calm patience of our God,
That waits to soothe our sorrows
  And lift our heaviest load, —
And gives us melodies of home,
  To cheer us on the road.

Above the money-changers,
  Above the toil and strife
Of all this fretting eagerness,
  With which the world is rife, —
Our Father keeps for us in store,
  An everlasting life !

Ah ! music softly pealing
   Through that sun-sifted air,
Your strains brought gifts of healing
   To many a heart-ache there ;
And men a moment stopped to praise,
   Who had no time for prayer.

A NEW DAY.

AS if already pulsed in every part,
 The beating of the ardent sun's deep heart,
The new Day waited on the verge of Dawn,
And wide before her stretched a boundless sea,
Fed from the fountains of Eternity.
Far streamed her pennons, tinged with rosy light,
Beyond the films of mist about her drawn.
Behind her hovered still reluctant Night,
A builder loath from labor to be gone.
One only star in steadfast silence kept
Its lover-vigil while the great world slept;
Till sudden bird-songs swept the dusk like flame,
And, launched on space, the bright creation came, —
A Day from God for freight of smiles and tears,
For childhood's joy, for dreams and hopes and fears.

THE TRAILING ARBUTUS.

A YEAR ago, in the sweet spring weather,
  We sought the trailing arbutus together.

Brushing the withered leaves aside,
And the long pine-needles, brown and dried,

We found the vine, with its glossy green,
And its clustering flowers coy between.

Over the waxen petals white
Hovered a blush as they met the light, —

Pure as the look a maiden wears
As forth she comes from her morning prayers.

I gathered the lovely things for you,
With the breath of the woods in their drops of dew;

And home we went by the common way,
With a halo around our holiday.

For we both had lost and we both had found
A something sweet on the forest ground.

And if your heart was exchanged for mine,
As we sought the blossoms beneath the pine,

The pine was far too high to hear
The words I whispered in your ear.

But the shy arbutus knew of the Yes,
That you let me seal with love's first kiss ;

And so this year, in the fair spring weather,
We will hunt for spring's sweet blooms together.

ICE–CROWNED.

GLANCING in armor of crystal,
   Splendid in serried array,
Blazing with marvellous beauty,
   Glittered the branches to-day, —
Sheathed by invisible fingers,
   Sparkling with opaline spray.

Bright, when the blossoms were weaving
   Spells for the wantoning bees ;
Rare, when the loves of the robins
   Quivered in song on the breeze ;
Never before such enchantment
   Wildered you, wonderful trees.

What though the glory shall vanish
   Swift as the thought of a dream !
Once to have worn it is rapture ;
   Days that are coming shall seem
Rich, for the memory of this one —
   Golden, triumphant, supreme !

Over your boughs interlacing,
   Clear to the tiniest stem,
Wavered the wand of the ice-king,
   Changing each drop to a gem, —
Amethyst, topaz, and ruby,
   Fit for his own diadem.

Crowned ! yet all night were ye moaning ;
   Wet with the rain, and forlorn, —
Tossed in the whirl of the tempest,
   Weary and faint for the morn ;
Touched by the rhythm of sunlight
   Into what peace are ye borne !

LILIES.

THE lilies, ah, the lilies !
    They stand superb in light,
In field and bank and garden fair,
    A wonder to the sight ;
So rich their royal scarlet is,
    So pure their stainless white !

Consider, then, the lilies,
    O heart of mine, to-day :
They neither toil nor spin, to win
    Their beautiful array ;
I would that thou couldst live a life
    So fearless-sweet as they.

They gather when the summer
    Her silver bugle thrills ;
When troop, to meet her shining feet,
    The bright, uncounted rills ;
And when the purple glories lie
    All softly o'er the hills.

Each in her place appointed,
    The lily dwells serene ;
She cares not though the thistle blow
    Anear her leaf of green ;
Her neighbors cannot vex her soul,
    For she was born a queen.

She fills the air with fragrance,
    She crowns the day with bloom ;
From dewy morn to darkling eve,
    Our shadows to illume,
She bears a torch, divinely fed,
    And smiles away our gloom.

Fair lilies, gentle teachers,
    Evangelists of love,
The word that bids me heed your voice
    Is spoken from above ;
Ye are the gracious gift of Him
    In whom our spirits move.

We too would wear unspotted
   The garments of the King,
Would have the royal perfume
   About our paths to cling,
And unto all beholders
   A lilied beauty bring.

THE OLD CHURCH.

IT lifteth its gray old spire from the heart of the busy
town,
Pointing the thoughts of the people from the things that
bind men down —

Up from toil and temptation, and struggle for daily bread,
To the blessed Father in heaven, to whom our prayers
are said, —

Who knoweth what we have need of before it passeth
our lips,
Who pitieth and forgiveth our frailty and our slips !

A century and a quarter dream-like has flitted away
Since they laid the stone in the corner, one sunny summer
day.

Grave men and stately matrons and rosy children stood,
While the minister sought a blessing for the church they
    built in the wood —

That thither, for peace and comfort, might throng from
    many lands
Those who should after worship in the house not made
    with hands.

As it rose in its fair proportions, higher from day to day,
In the shade of the forest round it, the children came to
    play !

To-day the birds are singing from their nests in the dusky
    eaves ;
Then shook their matins and vespers out from the
    rustling leaves.

Vanished the quiet forest !   In its place the restless town,
With its hive-like hum and bustle, its houses smoky and
    brown !

The church in its green enclosure has only room for
    graves,
And over the mossy tombstones the graceful willow waves !

Here sleep the men and women of a hundred years ago,
Folded in silent slumber, neath the sunlight and the snow.

Out from the grand old spire still tolls the bell for the
dead ;
Still merrily peals its music for the happy hearts of the wed.

From the ancient oaken pulpit the message of God is
given,
And from Sabbath to Sabbath are sinners pointed to hope
and heaven.

The mourner findeth comfort, the weary findeth calm ;
And the sorely wounded spirit is soothed with Gilead's
balm.

Here the stranger's eye may brighten as he sees the greet-
ing word :
" Ever the stranger is welcome in the dwelling of the
Lord ! "

And the rich and poor together to mingle worship come
As the children of One Father — all bound for one sweet
home.

Long may the dear old spire, from the heart of the busy
    town,
Lift the thought of the people from all that binds it
    down, —

From wealth they must leave behind them, when low they
    lie in the mold,
To the city whose walls are jasper, whose streets are paved
    with gold ;

Where we hope at last to gather, lifting our songs of praise,
Where never a shade shall darken the sunlight of our
    days ;

And no voices with tears along them shall tremble in the
    chord
Of the hallelujahs rising in that temple of the Lord.

SABBATH DAY.

A LITTLE aside from the sweep and whirl,
   The shifting splendor of swift Broadway,
Is a place where sounds but gently purl,
   And a spell of quiet invests the day.
There marbles are gleaming in beauty wrought,
   And rosy faces of children glow,
And the painter's vision hath shrined the thought
   Of tropical sunlight or polar snow.

There, late on a summer's afternoon,
   Till the shadowing twilight softly fell,
I lingered, reluctant to leave too soon
   A simple picture which pleased me well.
Steady and cheerful, strong and sweet,
   Was the womanly face that drew my gaze,
With a look which smiled my own to meet,
   A wonderful blending of prayer and praise.

'T was a dame of the Highlands, sturdy still,
　　Though youth had left her many a day,
And used to taking, with resolute will,
　　Her path to church in the good old way.
Whether sunlit mists to the mountains clung,
　　Or the tempest athwart them were driven wild,
She went to the kirk, where the psalms were sung,
　　Fearless and brave as an eager child.

I thought how often some trifle kept
　　Our dainty women from cushioned pews :
Too late, perhaps, in the morn they 've slept,
　　Or the hat is amiss, or tight the shoes ;
There 's the hint of rain in the clouded sky,
　　And the book and the easy-chair invite.
I thought as I gazed in the steadfast eye
　　Of the Highland mother, blithe and bright —

Little she cared for the bitter blast,
　　Or the swirl of the storm in her lifted face ;
She would win through its uttermost stress at last,
　　And endurance was hers, from a hardy race.
A narrow life in her lowly cot
　　She led, as she cared for barn and byre ;
But narrower far, where God is not,
　　Are lives which the loftiest men desire.

There 's something grand in the quiet way
　Yon strong soul passes, from sun to sun,
The week-day hours and the Sabbath-day
　Counting alike by duties done.
The breath of the hills in that picture fair,
　With the tangled heather bent and wet,
And the tranquil woman, amid it there,
　Are cordial and help to my spirit yet.

DINNA BIDE AWA'.

"DINNA bide awa',"
    The mither aft would say,
When, ere the nicht would fa',
    Her bairnies ran to play.
"The shades will sune grow lang,
    The lamps will lighted be,
Sae leave the merry thrang,
    Come hame an' bide wi' me."

Ah ! gentle mither voice,
    The warld hath muckle strife ;
Thy darlings hae nae choice,
    They maun hae griefs in life ;
But aye when mornin' wakes,
    An' aye when twilights fa',
Thy word the silence breaks,
    Wi' " Dinna bide awa'."

Frae that sweet hame aboon,
  The clouds and shadows gray,
The lamps are glistening on
  The rough and stony way.
Wha heeds that days are lang,
  Or cares for evil fate,
Wha yet shall hear the sang
  O' welcome at the gate?

The golden gate that stands
  Forever open wide,
Where in the best o' lands,
  We yet at hame shall bide, —
How tender on the ear,
  Its greetin' words will fa';
The Father's house is here,
  An' dinna bide awa'.

THE ARGIVE MOTHER.

ON the terse heroic pages
   Of the stately elder time,
Where the wisdom of the ages
  Lives in melody sublime,
I this story long ago
Read, the sunbeams dropping low,

Through the leaves of oak and maple,
  On the brown and ancient book,
With the scent of pear and apple,
  And the lapping of the brook,
And the vestal lilies white,
Each a separate delight.

'T was the Argive mother's story :
　She who, borne to Juno's feast
By her sons, her pride, her glory,
　Nobler none in west or east,
Lifted up her voice in prayer
To the goddess, crowned and fair.

"Give to these," so cried the mother,
　"These my darlings, I implore,
Some rich guerdon, like no other,—
　Make them joyful evermore :
Bless them, touch them, queenly heart,
With thine own divinest art."

Poured she then the choice libation
　Of the sacrificial wine.
Ah, the bursts of acclamation !
　Ah ! how bright the sun did shine !
Stole a whisper through the noon :
" Woman, granted is thy boon."

Turning, beautiful with gladness,—
　All her soul's ecstatic grace,
Beaming, burning, shaming sadness,
　Lighting ardently her face,—
Forth she stepped, her matron brow
Proud and calm as Juno's now.

As before a progress royal
    Parted all the eager throng,
And, to Juno's brightness loyal,
    Fed her heart with shout and song.
Still that whisper through the noon
Told her " Granted is thy boon."

.   .   .   .

" Are ye sleeping?   Waken !   Waken !
    First-born, twin-born sons of mine !
I for you in prayer have taken
    Pledge and vow at Juno's shrine.
Sorrow, pain, or creeping fears
Shall not blight your manly years.

" Waken !   Wherefore sleep in daylight?
    Ah ! " — a bitter wailing cry ;
Sudden, awful, hath the gray night
    Fallen from the radiant sky.
Is it thus hath Juno heard?
Keeps she so her plighted word?

Dead — both sons !   Nay, broken-hearted,
    Hapless mother, — 't was thy prayer
That no trial, poison-darted,
    Evermore their souls should bear.
They are glad, with gladness great,
Lifted far from evil fate.

Did the mother feel it — lonely,
　　Desolate, grown too early old?
It *was* Juno's answer; only
　　Prayer unheard had been less cold.
'T was a pitiless gift in sooth,
Emptied arms and blasted youth.

Do we dream how our petitions
　　Granted, might, like swords of wrath,
Sweep away the sweet conditions
　　And the mercies from our path, —
Leave us shorn of all our pride,
Fenceless, trampled, cast aside?

Do we know?　O dear compassion,
　　Gracious ruth, that bids us wait,
Though we mourn, in thankless fashion,
　　That the answers tarry late,
And, o'erwhelmed by waves of care,
Have no patience in our prayer!

CASTING THE FIRST VOTE.

FROM mountain homes engirdled
   By shadowy gloom of pines,
From hamlets whence the fisher's boat
Sets sail o'er stormful seas to float ;
   From darkling depth of mines,
A host come forth to cast their vote,
   A host in marshalled lines.

Clear-eyed, strong-limbed, and sturdy,
   These honest sons of toil, —
They hold the ballot like a prayer,
Uplifted through the fateful air,
   That none our land may spoil.
In their young manhood everywhere
   They rise to guard the soil.

From cloistered halls of study,
  From class-room and debate,
With chastened look and mien severe,
Another army draweth near,
  In patriot hope elate, —
The vote they drop, a pledge sincere
  To love and serve the State.

Up from the busy cities,
  From many a thronging street,
Come reinforcements brave and strong;
And, like the rhythm of a song,
  I hear their marching feet, —
To aid the weak, to right the wrong,
  Nor meanly to retreat.

God bless the pure endeavor,
  God guide the earnest thought;
God lead these youthful columns on,
Where only Freedom's fights are won,
  And Freedom's glory sought, —
Where Truth's light-bringers forward run,
  And Truth's brave deeds are wrought.

CHILDREN'S SLUMBER SONG.

ALL the lambs in all the folds are sleeping by their
    mothers ;
All the birds with golden wings have tucked their heads
    from sight ;
Far away and near at hand, let sisters wee, and brothers,
    Kiss, with lips like rosebuds cleft, and bid the world
    good-night.

All the stars in fields above shine out like jewelled flowers ;
    Wheresoe'er the flowers be, they fold their petals up ;
While silently and tenderly steal on the dreaming hours,
    When all the merry little ones have sipped the Lethe
    cup.

One by one, with soundless feet, go forth the slumber
    angels,
And sift the silver sand of rest o'er all the quiet land ;
Till cheeks are flushed and voices hushed, and, with their
    sweet evangels,
    The happy messengers have lulled each darling house-
    hold band.

PILGRIMS.

THERE 'S but the meagre crust, Love,
    There 's but the measured cup ;
On scanty fare we breakfast,
    On scanty fare we sup.
Yet be not thou discouraged,
    Nor falter on the way,
Since Wealth is for a life, Love,
    And Want is for a day.

Our robes are hodden gray, Love.
    Ah ! would that thine were white,
And shot with gleams of silver,
    And rich with golden light.
Yet care not thou for raiment,
    But climb, as pilgrims may,
Since Ease is for a life, Love,
    And Toil is for a day.

Our shelter oft is rude, Love ;
    We feel the chilling dew,
And shiver in the darkness
    Which silent stars shine through.
Yet shall we reach our palace,
    And there in gladness stay,
Since Home is for a life, Love,
    And Travel for a day.

The heart may sometimes ache, Love,
    The eyes grow dim with tears ;
Slow glide the hours of sorrow,
    Slow beats the pulse of fears.
Yet patience with the evil,
    For, though the good delay,
Still Joy is for a life, Love,
    And Pain is for a day.

NEW–MOWN HAY.

SWEET, oh sweet, from the fields to-day
   Wafts the breath of the new-mown hay.

Sewing away in a happy dream,
I sit in the porch with my long white seam.

The very silence is like a tune,
Sung to the golden afternoon.

While the house is still, and the meadows lie
Fast asleep 'neath the radiant sky.

Only at intervals, now and then,
I hear the farmer call to his men.

And the farmer's voice is dear to me
As ever a mortal voice can be.

You may talk of the love of youth and maid,
Of two in childhood, perhaps, who played

Together by rill and fount and tree,
Till their hearts had grown one heart to be ;

You may tell of the loyal faith and life
Of the husband dear and the gentle wife ;

But the widowed mother leans closest on
The tender strength of her only son.

Ah ! what if that farmer of mine one day
Should seek him a bride, as well he may,

And bring her home !   Would I be loath,
Mother and friend, to live for both?

For somehow the scent of the new-mown hay
Carries me back to a far-off day,

When my silver hair was in waves of brown,
When my bashful glances kept looking down,

And swift to my cheek, in a sudden red,
Mounted the blush, at a soft word said.

Truly the days of my youth were sweet,
Ere the path was rough to my toiling feet.

Truly the morning of life was blest,
And yet in sooth is the evening best ;

For I 've learned the lesson that joys must fly,
And the proudest hopes, like flowers, die.

But God abides in his heaven, and he
Will never forget to care for me.

Sweet, oh sweet, is the new-mown hay,
Wafting its breath from the fields to-day.

Sweet is the golden afternoon,
With its silence rhythmic as a tune,

And dear to the soul is the calm content
Of hours in grateful trusting spent.

A GARDEN OF SPICES.

ALL odors sweet of spice and balm,
　　All breath of flower and vine,
To-day have found their way, O Lord,
　　To these fair fields of thine.

The earth is radiant as a bride
　　In broidered garments dressed;
She wears thy glory like a gem
　　Upon her happy breast.

From cliff and dell a song goes up
　　In every wind that blows;
We hear it in the morning's joy,
　　And in the night's repose.

Each bird that pours his gladness out,
　　Each moth that rustles by,
Hath part within the strain of praise
　　Clear thrilling to the sky.

Lord, pardon us for little faith,
 Revive our drooping love ;
Still pardon us, if weak and faint
 The hymns we lift above.

Within thy summer garden we
 Oft walk in winter's gloom.
Oh, let the sun that warms the sod,
 Our shadowed souls illume.

Then shall we bring forth fruit for thee, —
 We, joined to heavenly Vine ;
And still our grateful song shall be,
 That we, dear Lord, are thine.

A HAPPY NEW YEAR.

ALL robed in ethereal whiteness
    Glides in the first morn of the year ;
And round it a wonderful brightness
    Is floating, in token of cheer.
The glad and the sorrowful-hearted
    Alike look for blessings to be,
Ere it pass to the ages departed,
    And lost in eternity's sea.

Already the year which has left us
    Seems old as the Pyramids are.
It taught or enriched or bereft us,
    Yet now hath receded as far —
As wholly hath lessened and faded
    From vision, and melted from clasp, —
As the years which Rome's purple o'ershaded,
    When the world was a toy in her grasp.

Even yesterday past groweth hoary,
　Allied to traditions of eld,
Partaking the gloom and the glory
　The cycles uncounted have held.
And the new year, with breathless to-morrows,
　With raptures and yearnings and sighs,
Defeats and disasters and sorrows,
　Has Eden's lost youth in our eyes.

Not new, like the coin golden glinting,
　Completed, that falls from the mint, —
Nor new, like the broidery hinting
　Of splendor in ever fresh tint, —
But new, like the child onward gazing
　At life all before it unknown,
Like the prince when the vassals are raising
　Their banners in love round his throne.

No word of its words hath been spoken,
　No deed of its deeds hath been done ;
Nor the bread of its benisons broken,
　Nor its battles in bravery won.
Still tarry its songs for the singers,
　Still slumber its manifold looms ;
Its bells are yet waiting the ringers,
　And vacant are standing its tombs.

Though it bear for us wisdom or folly,
   In silence it utters no sign;
Through our garlands of cedar and holly
   There murmurs no message divine, —
Save this, that with loyal endeavor,
   And heart of all enmity clear,
Who welcomes it gayly may ever
   Look forth on a Happy New Year.

THANKSGIVING.

SWEET was the song of the robin,
  Blithe was the hum of the bee,
In the day when the drift of the blossom
  Was light as the foam of the sea.
Then deeply was cloven the furrow,
  And gayly they scattered the seed,
Who trusted that rainfall and sunshine
  Would surely be given at need.

The robin hath flown to the tropic,
  The honey-bee flitteth no more ;
The reaper hath garnered the harvest,
  And the fruit and the nuts are in store.
The flame hath died out on the maples,
  We tread on the loose-lying leaves,
And the corn, that was sturdy and stalwart,
  Is gathered and bound into sheaves.

And sweeter than music of springtime,
  And fuller of jubilant mirth,
Are the strong-tided chorals o'erflowing
  From hearts where thanksgiving has birth.
The songs of the home and the altar,
  The gladness of children at play,
And the dear love of households united
  Are blending in praises to-day.

For pasture-lands folded with beauty,
  For plenty that burdened the vale,
For the wealth of the teeming abundance,
  And the promise too royal to fail,
We lift to the Maker our anthems,
  But none the less cheerily come
To thank him for bloom and fruition,
  And the happiness crowning the home.

Oh, the peace on the brow of the father,
  The light in the mother's clear eyes,
The lilt in the voices of maidens
  Who walk under dream-curtained skies,
The dance in the feet of the wee ones,
  The sparkle and shine in the air !
The year has no time like Thanksgiving ;
  A truce to our fretting and care !

Sweet was the song of the robin,
    Blithe was the hum of the bee,
In the day when the drift of the blossom
    Was light as the foam of the sea ;
But sweeter the silence of autumn,
    Dearer the tender refrain,
When the aftermath waveth no longer,
    And rest comes to mountain and plain.

BAYARD TAYLOR.

A PLAINTIVE monotone of pain
  Sighs through our land, bereft to-day,
A dissonance within the strain
  So lately set to measures gay.
We mourn for one too early lost
  From life and love and labors high, —
Gone, when his country prized him most,
  And dead beneath a foreign sky.

From Norway's shadowy groves of pine,
  From far Palmyra's ruins gray,
From cloud-capped Alp and Apennine,
  From ocean isle and rock-girt bay,
Come notes to swell the tearful rune —
  Which trees and winds and surges blend —
For him, with pilgrim staff and shoon,
  Who made each leaf and flower a friend.

His was the poet's heaven-born fire,
   And his the harp of troubadour;
With hand of strength he swept the lyre,
   The master's touch, so swift and sure.
No stain obscured his well-earned fame;
   His manhood's honor whitely shone;
And ever, as we spoke his name,
   We proudly thought " He is our own."

A youth, he sought with eager hope
   The busy city's crowded ways.
What doors before his feet should ope!
   What dreams grow real at his gaze!
The " Open Sesame " he tried
   Had magic in it as of old;
The world is hard, the world is wide,
   But toil and truth possess its gold.

To-day the Muses veil their eyes,
   As, hushed around that laurelled brow,
The brave, the beautiful, the wise,
   In stress of deep bereavement bow;
But, in Valhalla's stately seats,
   The glad immortals haste to give
Such welcome as he only meets
   Whose royal work shall ever live.

IN MY NEIGHBOR'S GARDEN.

IN the bound of mine own enclosure
    The flowers are fair to see ;
But the rose in my neighbor's garden
    Is fairer than all to me.

So white and slender and stately,
    So gemmed with sparkling dew,
This rose that blooms for another,
    Is the sweetest ever that grew.

My heart to its grace and beauty
    Goes forth as to a shrine ;
And I sigh to its mystical fragrance —
    " If it were only mine ! "

And yet if not my neighbor,
    But I, in fee and thrall,
Held all that marvellous glory
    On the other side of the wall,

I might, perhaps, grow weary
  Of its royal pomp and grace,
And love with my love some daisy
  With a shy, uplifted face.

For since the gates of Eden
  Were shut on Adam and Eve,
The flowers we have are never
  So sweet as the flowers we leave;

And rich within my garden
  Though many a flower might be,
The rose that bloomed for another
  Might seem the best to me.

THE HONEY-BIRD.

THE honey-bird, my children,
  Lives far and far away,
Where burning suns are beating
  Through Afric's tropic day.

There, deep in sombre forests,
  Are colonies of bees,
Who hive their golden honey
  In hearts of hollow trees.

The hunters seek to find it;
  Their eyes are sharp and bright;
Their forms are lithe and agile;
  Their steps are quick and light.

But they might seek forever,
  Forever and a day,
Unless to find the honey
  A bird should show the way, —

A lovely bird that flashes
  With sudden arrow-flight,
And then, returning, utters
  A cry of rare delight:

A cheerful " Follow ! Follow ! "
  As if it fain would say,
" The bees and I are neighbors,
  And I can tell the way."

That ringing " Follow ! Follow ! "
  Allures the hunters on
Until their quest is ended,
  The feast of nectar won.

And which hath sweeter promise,
  The honey-bird or bee ;
I tell you, little children,
  It is not plain to me.

We cannot all make honey;
　But some can find it out,
And show its hive to others, —
　A gracious thing, no doubt.

And, in this world of thickets,
　And tangles, if you please,
One likes to know the birds who
　Are neighbors to the bees.

OCTOBER.

WHERE the gentle West Wind sigheth,
    And the South Wind low replieth;
Where the faint blush — stealing through
Mornings, bridal-gemmed with dew —
Hath a trembling glow and tender;
Where the noons are rich with splendor,
And the sunsets, soft and golden,
Linger on the mountains olden, —
There, enchanting, fair, serene,
Dwells October, like a queen.

Hers are slow, bewitching hours,
Couched on fragrant, blooming flowers:
Tasselled salvia's scarlet fringes;
Gay lantana's radiant tinges;
Eastern lilies dark and stately;
Purple heliotrope that, lately,
Spent its lavish sweetness where
Roses perfumed all the air;

Fluted dahlias deeply dyed ;
Asters bright on every side,
Standing steadfast floral wardens
In our separated gardens,
Floating, mist-like, o'er the hedges
Rural, which the sumach edges
With its vivid plumes of fire,
Torch-like raised o'er branch and brier.

Hers — our sunlit, clear October —
Is the oak-leaf's tinting sober ;
Dusk against the sky, and solemn,
Lifts the strong old oak its column ;
Hers, the maple's yellow flashing,
And the linden's crimson dashing ;
Hers, the elm with spreading glory,
Hers, the ripe year's finished story, —
All the wealth of freighted sheaves,
All the songs of harvest eves.

Trees, that whitened into blossom ;
Trees, that rocked, in ample bosom,
Mated birds and humming bees,
And the soft vibrating breeze ;

Trees, that bore the peach and apple ;
Trees, that whirlwinds sought to grapple, —
Surely when your tasks are over,
And the Autumn, like a lover,
With the kisses of his mouth,
Sweet and wooing as the South,
Bids you glow in pomp supernal,
Richer than your beauty vernal, —
Surely in these dreamful days,
Amber-sealed, in silver haze,
Ye are joyous and content,
'Neath the glorious firmament.

Like to Aaron's rod that budded,
Till the house of God was flooded
With its almond-fragrance — white
As the stars that shine at night,
Is one flower that lingers fair,
Filling the October air
With its subtle sense of sweet,
Till the zephyrs seem to beat
Phantom music to its time.
Pure as frost-work's crystal rime
Is the waxen tuberose.
Tired eyes that droop and close,

Weary hands that, folded, rest,
Silent on the quiet breast,
O'er your sacred peace in death
Pours the rapture of its breath.
Dipped in snow, the brush that paints
This white flower of the saints !

Shall we grieve that birds are winging
Far to other lands, and singing
Farewell notes upon their way?
Shall we shadow this bright present,
Rainbow-tinted, iridescent,
With that ghostly future day, —
That impending chance that may
Bring us pain, or gloom, or sorrow?
Rather let our spirits borrow
Gladness from the rich libation,
Nectar-brimmed at coronation
Of this loveliest month of all,
Diamond-threaded, of the Fall.

For the gentle West Wind sigheth,
And the tender South replieth ;
And the faint blush, stealing through
Morning's bridal veil of dew,

Hath a glow surpassing other ;
And the noon is like a mother,
With her fair hands full of treasure ;
And the sunsets, in their pleasure,
Bathe with glory, rich and golden,
Valley slope and mountains olden, —
And enchanting, rare, serene,
Reigns October, like a queen.

MOTHER-COMFORT.

FRIEND, upon whose golden tresses
 Frost of time begins to fall,
Though your heart is like the mellow
 Fruit beside the garden wall,
Tell me !   Do you not remember
 Sunny days of long ago,
When the world was full of beauty,
 Full of sparkle and of glow, —
When one gentle face was fairer
 Far than artist e'er could paint,
Face that wears in reverent memory
 Aureole circlet of a saint ?

When the little heart was troubled
 Sometimes, in those distant days,
Grieving o'er a brittle plaything,
 Sad, for blame instead of praise ;
When the rain of tears was falling,
 And the passion of the hour

Beat against the wounded spirit,
    Like the storm against a flower, —
Then the comfort of the mother,
    Soft as sunshine, always stole
Through the tumult and the turmoil,
    Bringing peace unto the soul.

Never accents were so tender,
    Never touch so light and strong,
Never voice in speech so cadenced
    To the measure of a song,
And beneath her dewy kisses,
    And her murmured-cooing words,
And the magic of her patience,
    Hearts were hushed like nestling birds,
That the mother-breast hath sheltered,
    And the mother-wings enfold,
While the cloud is on the midnight,
    And the wind is in the wold.

Ah! Those days were long and happy,
    Though a trifle could obscure
All their brightness; yet their troubles
    Just a single kiss could cure.

Then the peril and the danger
   Stayed outside the door of home,
And we felt so safe by mother, —
   Dared the wildest grief to come, —
Careless of its utmost menace,
   When the summer's silver fleece,
Trembled o'er the radiant heaven,
   Blue and luminous with peace.

Now no word of all the Scripture
   Thrills a sweeter chord than this,
Stirs a richer retrospection
   Of the soul's experienced bliss,
Than this promise, where the Spirit
   Strengthens weak and timid faith
With assurance of His comfort:
   " As the mother comforteth."

Oh ! when mother-lips no longer
   Kiss the sudden tears away,
When the idol of our loving
   Can with us no longer stay,
Needs the heart bereft to murmur,
   Bowing in the dust alone,
When the Christ will stoop to send it,
   Such sweet blessing from the throne?

MARTYRS.

MY child, whose soul is like a flame
    Within a crystal altar-lamp,
Bends o'er an ancient book, its name
    Obscured by mildew damp;

And, tracing down the yellow leaves,
    Where quaint and crooked letters stand,
Her breath comes quick, her bosom heaves,
    Hard shuts the eager hand.

"Mamma," — I meet the lifted eyes
    That, softened, shine through gathering tears —
" God surely gives them in the skies,
    For all those dreadful years,

" Some sweeter thing than others have,
    To comfort after so much pain;
But, tell me, could we be as brave
    Through fire and rack and chain?

" I 'm glad there are no martyrs now."
  Blithe rings the voice and positive.
" Ah, Love," my own heart answers low,
  " The martyrs ever live.

" A royal line in silk and lace,
  Or robed in serge and hodden gray,
With fearless step and steadfast face
  They tread the common way.

" Than dungeon bolt, or folding blaze,
  Their cross unseen may heavier press,
And none suspect, through smiling days,
  Their utmost bitterness."

" Some sweet thing surely God must keep
  To comfort," said my little one ;
" They thank Him now if tender sleep
  Comes when the day is done."

God's angel, Sleep, with manifold
  Soft touches, smoothing brows of care,
Dwells not beyond the gates of gold,
  Because no night is there.

MERCEDES.

O LOVELIEST lily, severed from the stem
    Of rich sweet-breathing life, and frozen cold !
O fair young Queen, whom earthly diadem
    May wreathe no longer ! Brilliant story told,
Glad years all numbered, — 't was a ruthless dart
That in thy summer's morning pierced thy heart.

So late we listened to the bridal bells
    Which sent their silver peals across the main,
And dreamed we heard this voice amid their swells, —
    " New hope, new peace, a new day's dawn for Spain."
So late Madrid, along rejoicing ways,
Sent ringing forth its many-chorded praise !

Who is not glad when manhood's stately strength,
    To woman's flower-like bloom is proudly wed ?
Alfonso and Mercedes : through the length
    And breadth of lands remote the tidings sped ;
And simple swains and cottage maids in prayer
Sought blessings on the twain so brave and fair.

And now the banners droop, the roses pale,
   The soft gray olives shiver in the sun,
The summer breezes, quivering, moan and wail ;
   Sadly the golden rivers, as they run
Through shining valleys or by mountains hoar,
Bear on the tale : " The dear Queen lives no more."

She lives no more ! Yet shall her stately grace
   Still like a perfume through all time abide.
The beauty of her innocent, sweet face
   Be unforgotten, and with tender pride
The poets of her people speak her name,
And wreathe with songs her clear and stainless fame.

Lives she no more ? Ah, victor over Death,
   She met him tranquil, calm ; and no eclipse
Dimmed the high courage of her steadfast faith.
   She held the crucifix to whitening lips,
That, smiling, seemed to frame, " Thy will be done,"
Till darkness hid her from our earthly sun.

O Love supreme ! O Love that never yet
   In sharpest hour of need forsook thine own !
An aureole of light henceforth is set
   Above the shadows of that vacant throne.
Within Escurial's gloom her dust shall lie,
But Love has borne her to the upper sky.

THE FOUNDLING.

THERE 'S the glimmer of dew on the bending grass ;
　There 's arrowy light from the sunny sky,
Where the soft fleece clouds, as they meet and pass,
　Like the pictured sails in a dream go by ;
And, herself as fair as a morn of May,
The maiden walks in the early day.

Hark !　What was that from the tangled hedge
　A little way back?　'T was a cry of pain,
And she paused at the pasture's rippling edge,
　And listened.　It came to her ear again, —
The moan of a wee lost lamb, distressed,
And soon she was clasping it to her breast.

Wrapping it close in her mantle's fold,
　And over it grieving with gentle eyes.
" Poor little wanderer, faint and cold,
　Another time will you not be wise, —
Stay by the flock in a safer place?"
She seems to say with her tender face.

That pitiful face reveals a heart
   With room to cherish all helpless things ;
Hers, you may guess, is the magic art
   Which everywhere healing and comfort brings.,
Deft are her fingers with womanly skill,
And womanly sweet is her gracious will.

The wee white lamb has forgotten fear ;
   Content he lies in the loving arms,
Which cradle him soft in a hemisphere
   Of fond caresses and placid charms.
Frightened and chilled was the waif last night,
But love has found him at morning's light.

STRAWBERRY TIME.

WHEN the strawberry, ripening, blushes
　　To meet the sweet looks of the sun,
Then faintly the fair laurel flushes ;
　　Then gayly the eager winds run
To tell, upon hillside and meadow,
　　The coming of festival days,
While out from his nest in the shadow
　　The bird pours his jubilant lays.

The pasture-lands dimple with clover,
　　The buttercups dazzle and shine ;
The wide fields of summer brim over
　　With dreams of a perfume divine ;
And forth go the children as merry,
　　As harvesters seeking for sheaves,
With bright eyes discerning the berry,
　　A ruby mid emerald leaves.

Brown-handed, sun-freckled, they linger
  To eat the sweet globes while they pick ;
What care they for stain on the finger,
  So ripe is the treasure, and thick ;
Like music their innocent laughter
  Rings out o'er their frolic and haste ;
Ah ! never will berries hereafter
  Hold nectar so rich to the taste.

Hereafter, when shrill voices cry them,
  Discordant, through streets of the town,
And gravely they bargain and buy them,
  Their value in silver pay down, —
Yet haply remembering childhood,
  They 'll say, as at evening they eat :
" The berries we found in the wildwood,
  Unsugared, were surely more sweet."

And yet can the dear, evanescent,
  Illusive, full charm of the fruit
Be known to the children whose present
  Suffices unto them ?   The root
Of every glad hour of pleasure
  Must grow, deeply struck, in the past ;
And so is our berry a treasure
  Less prized at the first than at last.

For now as the shy things are blushing
　　Low down mid their leaves on the ground,
As the delicate laurels are flushing
　　On hillock and meadow and mound, —
We, working and weary with labor,
　　Shut in among houses of brick,
Hear sounds, as of pipe and of tabor,
　　From fields where the berries are thick.

THE ENGLISH FARM–LABORER'S SUNDAY.

THE winds are sweet that sweep to-day
    O'er miles of tilth and fallow,
And clear the ring from far away
    Of Sabbath chimes that hallow
And set the morning by itself,
    Serenest of the seven.
" Take down the Bible from the shelf,
    And read the words of heaven."

Did some one speak? The house is still ;
    Yet if a voice had spoken,
Not swifter could the low " I will "
    Have sent responsive token.
The old man bends above the page,
    With reverent eyes that linger,
While traces out its counsel sage
    His slow and patient finger.

Flows on the stately Hebrew psalm
   In grand heroic measure ;
It floods his soul with waves of calm,
   It fills his heart with pleasure :
" Commit thy way unto the Lord,
   And trust His loving-kindness ;
He 'll keep thee fast in watch and ward,
   And smite thy foes with blindness.

" His rain upon thy pasture-land
   Shall fall in gentle showers ;
His sun shall rise in beauty grand
   On orchard, grain, and flowers.
Though all thy loved should leave thy side,
   Thou shalt be never lonely,
For near thee will the Lord abide,
   If thou wilt serve Him only."

So, little learned in human lore,
   Nor skilled in disputation,
The simple peasant leans the more
   Upon the great salvation ;
In honest duty spends his days,
   And, friendly with his neighbor,
He sends to God the highest praise
   Through self-denying labor.

To him how dear the Sabbath rest !
  How more than dear the Bible !
In childlike faith his life is blessed ;
  And vain were skeptic's libel,
To shake the trust, sublimely strong,
  By which he holds on heaven,
And makes his lowly life a song
  Each day in all the seven.

A TWILIGHT MEMORY.

AT fall of night, when shadows gray
Enfold the feet of fading day,

Or on the far horizon's rim,
The rain-clouds gather vast and dim,

From some vague coast of memory,
A childhood scene returns to me.

I see my mother, sweet and fair,
Her gentle face 'neath shining hair.

I see myself, her little one,
With pensive looks, when day is done.

Uncertain what the dark may bring,
I nestle 'neath my mother's wing;

And even there, by fears possessed,
My trembling heart is not at rest.

A tender voice, I hear it yet,
Bids: " Light the lamps for Margaret."

And swift the cheery rays are poured
O'er curtained room and smiling board.

However thick the shadows meet
To-day around my weary feet,

No mother's presence at my side
Is strong to comfort, bless, and guide.

The dear one, lifted out of sight,
Dwells evermore in Love's own light;

But tones my heart can ne'er forget,
Above me sound in blessing yet;

And one by one, like stars that rise
Serene amid the steadfast skies,

The lamps of faith their glow divine
Diffuse around this life of mine,

And, sheltered e'en when storms are wild,
I dwell a safe and happy child.

"MY LORD AND MY GOD."

'TWAS evening and the doors were shut,
   No bar was that to him
Who came in kingly silence through
   The twilight growing dim.
In tones as tender as the dew,
He blessed them : " Peace be unto you."

It was the Master's loving word,
   The Master's form they knew ;
And nearer to the risen Lord
   The glad disciples drew.
What hope was in their hearts that hour !
What glory in his wondrous power !

His eyes in matchless pity dwelt
   On one reluctant face,
On one who knew not all the bliss
   Of full-believing grace.
That soul still fettered fast with doubt,
The love of Jesus singled out.

" Behold," said Christ, " these wounds of mine ;
   Feel where the nails were driven."
Ah, swift he knew the voice divine !
   His heart with love was riven ;
And leaped like flame his answering word :
" I know thee now, — my God, my Lord."

Then soft from Jesus' lips there fell
   A thought exceeding sweet ;
Let age to age its message tell,
   Its tenderness repeat ·
" Thou hast believed, for thou hast seen,
Blessed are they who have not seen,

And yet have trusted."   We rejoice,
   Dear Lord, and bless thy name ;
How sacred was that time when first
   To us that insight came,
And we beheld thee, crucified, —
Thy pierced hands, thy riven side.

Yet, seeing not the cross alone,
   Our eyes were lifted high ;
We knew thee sitting on the throne,
   We felt thee drawing nigh ;
And all our doubts were hushed to peace,
And from their chains we had release.

THE BETTER LIFE.

FROM silken cords of earth's delight,
　From iron chains of care,
O set us free when, in thy sight,
　Dear Lord, we kneel in prayer !

Forbid that dreams of ease and cheer,
　Or transient thoughts of pride,
Should make an alien atmosphere,
　To drift us from thy side.

Forgive if moaning discontent
　In unbelief complains ;
Forgive if when our hearts are rent
　We think but of their pains.

Still come thyself in darkest hours,
　And cleave the gloom with rays
So bright that all our grateful powers
　Shall turn from grief to praise.

Still consecrate our joyful times
　With bliss beyond compare,
While faith the spirit's strength sublimes,
　And robes of light we wear.

Oh lift us to the better life !
　These shadows come and go ;
But where thou art above the strife,
　The winds of heaven blow.

HITHERTO.

TO bluest skies that arch the way
　　I lift my thankful eyes to-day.
The sunlight falls, a golden tide,
O'er airy forests, green and wide ;
Pure odors drift the morning through,
And God has led me hitherto.

Sweet flower-perfumes thrill the air,
As if from censer swung at prayer ;
And sweeter fragrance fills my life
With all my Father's goodness rife ;
He gives me roses after rue,
And he has kept me hitherto.

What joy to take his guiding hand,
To trust, if not to understand, —
To rest through change and toil and tears
On him, whose grand eternal years
In ever living youth are new,
And cry, " He leads me hitherto."

Though other days have left their trace
Of weariness upon my face ;
Though sometimes from my harp the tone
Hath been a *miserere* moan ;
Yet God is good ; 't is his to do,
And mine to follow hitherto.

Though days to come may often be
With burdens crowded full for me ;
Though hope deferred may cast a shade
Across my spirit ; undismayed
I 'll meet them, one by one, for through
Such days He brought me hitherto.

No darkest night shall ever hide
This beacon, flaming o'er the tide ;
My life shall have a sweet refrain ;
For, victor over grief and pain,
I bless the Lord, whose mercies new
Have helped and cheered me hitherto.

THE HEAVEN-SIDE.

THE sky was soft with tender blue,
  As heaven itself were shining through,
And far above our restless world
Its bannered peace was wide unfurled.

The distant mountains' purple line
Was bathed in splendor all divine,
And seemed the valley's cup to brim
With waves of beauty to the rim.

The very wind was soft and sweet
That rocked the grass-blades at our feet,
And gently did the zephyrs blow
Across the buckwheat's billowy snow.

When lo, a change ! The tranquil sky
Grew dark, — the thick clouds drifted by ;
Like battled hosts in war's array,
Their vengeful ranks assault the day !

And grim and sullen; fold on fold,
They hide the summer's shining gold,
Till wood and field and wayside path
Are menaced in their stormy wrath.

Still o'er them soft that tender blue,
With heaven's brightness gleaming through,
All steadfast, radiant, undismayed,
Too lifted up to be afraid.

And while we shivered in the gray
Thick-falling gloom that wrapped the day,
Lo, touched by spears of sunny light,
The clouds were edged with sparkling white !

Ah ! looked on from the heaven-side,
They surely must be glorified,
And where God sees them, floating fair,
Seem isles of peace in upper air.

A VESPER SONG.

THE clouds of the sunset, fold on fold,
    Are purple and tawny, and edged with gold.

Soft as the silence after a hymn
Is the hush that falls as the light grows dim,

And the phantom feet of the shadows glide
To the maple-tops and the river's tide.

Not the thought of a sound is heard,
Till the dusk is thrilled by a hidden bird

That suddenly sings, as the light grows dim,
Its wonderful, passionate vesper hymn.

Sweet as the voice of an angel's call,
Sent to me from the jasper wall,

Is the music poured from that tiny throat,
A message of comfort in every note.

I know not where, in the leafy tree,
The dear little warbler's home may be,

Nor care I to find by a thoughtful quest
Its cunningly woven castled nest.

The singer was less to my heart to-night
Than the song he sent through the parting light.

Its overflow of a joy intense
Came unto me like a recompense,

For the undertone of an aching care
That had chilled my praise and chained my prayer.

There are in this world, where God is King,
Some who have nothing to do but sing;

Some who are all too blithe to keep
Pent up the voice of their rapture deep,

Though, it may be, low under waves of pain
They found the pearl of their purest strain.

Listening, we have naught to say
Concerning, to them, the Master's way,

Only this : it was surely best,
Since it taught them songs so full of rest ;

And this : that never a folding wing
Should cover a breast that was meant to sing,

And show the path to a lighted ark,
Perhaps to some one lost in the dark.

A RAINY DAY.

ALL day, against the window pane,
   The fitful dashing of the rain
Keeps up in dreary monotone
A minor music of its own, —
A weary moan of restless pain,
This chorded anthem of the rain.

My tired heart within me hears,
Too tired to-day for easeful tears,
And well interprets every sound
From sobbing sky and barren ground.
Like one who from the organ-keys,
Awakens threaded harmonies,
To fit in pauses of the strain
Another sings, I list the rain,
And try, through woven words of mine,
Its cadenced melody to twine.

All day it falls on little beds
That pillow softly baby heads,
From mother's tender nursing gone,
While yet her life was in its dawn.
Alas, how many a mother feels
The coldness of each drop that steals
Through that green coverlet that lies
Between her darling and her eyes !

All day it shuts the cheerful sun
From many a longing, lonely one.
No sparkling rift of heaven's blue
Breaks regnant all its mystery through ;
No golden radiance cleaves a way
Through close-set banks of vapor gray,
Slow-beating on the darkened pane
All day, the sleet, the storm, the rain !

Yet think, impatient soul of mine,
That somewhere still the sun must shine,
That somewhere other hearts are glad,
And days are not forlorn and sad,
And that God's benedictions still
Fall from stern lips of seeming ill.

In memory's light these drops may be
Like glittering amethysts to thee,
And all thy being yet may bless
His patient care and tenderness,
Who bids thee trust Him, not in vain,
For days clear shining after rain.

A MASQUERADE.

A LITTLE old woman before me
    Went slowly down the street,
Walking as if aweary
    Were her feeble tottering feet.

From under her old poke-bonnet
    I caught a gleam of snow,
And her waving cap-string floated
    Like a pennon to and fro.

In the folds of her rusty mantle,
    Sudden her footstep caught,
And I sprang to keep her from falling
    With a touch as quick as thought.

When, under the old poke-bonnet,
    I saw a winsome face,
Framed in with the flaxen ringlets
    Of my wee daughter Grace.

Mantle and cap together
　　Dropped off at my very feet,
And there stood the little fairy, —
　　Beautiful, blushing, sweet.

Will it be like this, I wonder,
　　When at last we come to stand
On the golden, gleaming pavement
　　Of the blessèd, blessèd land?

Losing the rusty garments
　　We wore in the years of Time,
Shall our better selves spring backward
　　Serene in a youth sublime?

Instead of the shapes that hid us,
　　And made us old and gray,
Shall we get our child-hearts back again,
　　With a brightness that will stay?

I thought — and my little daughter
　　Slipped her dimpled hand in mine.
" I was only playing," she whispered,
　　" That I was ninety-nine."

THE RIVER.

FAR up on the mountain the river begins, —
    I saw it, a thread in the sun.
Then it grew to a brook, and, through dell and
      through nook,
  It dimpled and danced in its fun.

A ribbon of silver, it sparkled along
  Over meadows besprinkled with gold ;
With a twist and a twirl, and a loop and a curl,
  Through the pastures the rivulet rolled.

Then on to the valleys it leaped and it laughed,
  Till it stronger and stiller became ;
On its banks the tall trees rocked their boughs in
      the breeze,
  And the lilies were tapers aflame.

The children threw pebbles, and shouted with glee
    At the circles they made in the stream ;
And the white fisher-boat, sent so lightly afloat,
    Drifted off like a sail in a dream.

Deep-hearted, the mirth of its baby-life past,
    It toiled for the grinding of corn ;
Its shores heard the beat of the lumberman's feet,
    His raft on its current was borne.

At inlet and cove, where its harbors were fair,
    Vast cities arose in their pride,
And the wealth of their streets came from beautiful
        fleets,
    Forth launched on its affluent tide.

The glorious river swept on to the sea,
    The sea that engirdles the land ;
But I saw it begin in a thread I could spin,
    Like a cobweb of silk, in my hand.

And I thought of the river that flows from the throne,
    Of the love that is deathless and free, —
Of the grace of his peace that shall ever increase,
    Christ-given to you and to me.

Far up on the mountain, and near to the sky,
  The cup full of water is seen,
That is brimmed till its tide carries benisons wide
  Where the dales and the meadows are green.

Is thy soul like a cup?   Let its little be given,
  Not stinted nor churlish, to One
Who will fill thee with love, and his faithfulness prove,
  And bless thee in shadow and sun.

A MAPLE LEAF.

SO bright in death I used to say,
    So beautiful through frost and cold !
A lovelier thing I know to-day,
    The leaf is growing old,
And wears in grace of duty done,
The gold and scarlet of the sun.

"EVEN SO, COME."

COME, Lord Jesus !
    The days are long, the nights are slow,
The pulse of life beats faint and low ;
The bloom is gone from flower and tree,
What can we do but wait for thee ?

    Come, Lord Jesus !
When youth was glad with song and love
And halcyon was the sky above,
When light the step, the spirit free,
Then less our hearts cried out for thee !

    Come, Lord Jesus !
Ah, voice that soundeth in the room !
Ah, Face Divine that breaks the gloom !
O tones that chide our strange unrest,
And bid us lean upon thy breast.

Come, Lord Jesus !
" Yes, child of mine, I come to thee,
But thou art all too blind to see ;
That pain and loss and ruth and rift
May each be my most gracious gift."

Come, Lord Jesus !
Come as thou wilt, in peace, in strife,
But with us stay in death and life,
Reveal thyself to eyes that ache,
And bless us for thy own dear sake.
Even so, come.

THE EVER–OPEN WAY.

I SOMETIMES like, when all my way seems barred,
 To mind me of the story told of one,
Whose faith the dawn of Britain's freedom starred
 Ere yet had beamed the rising of the sun.

Brave Cuthbert who, from tending of the sheep
 On wind-swept hillsides bleak, near Lammermoor,
Went forth the Master's scattered flock to keep,
 And preach his love who says, " I am the Door."

Once, tossed upon an angry boiling sea,
 His boat was dashed upon a dreary shore.
Heart-sick, and like to die, his comrades three
 Cried : " Cuthbert, let us perish — hope is o'er,

" The furious tempest shuts the water-path ;
 The snow-storm blinds us on the bitter land."
" Now wherefore, friends, have ye so little faith ? "
 God's servant said ; and, stretching forth his hand,

He lifted up his reverent eyes, and spake :
  " I thank thee, Lord, the way is open there !
No storm above our heads in wrath shall break,
  And shut the heavenward path of love and prayer."

Sweet to me comes old Cuthbert's word to-day ;
  Sweet is the thought that Christ is always near ;
I seek him by the ever-open way,
  Nor yield my courage to a shuddering fear.

The storm may darken over land and sea,
  But step by step with Christ I walk along ;
Dear Christ, the storm and sun are both of thee,
  And thou thyself art still my strength and song.

MOTHER'S WORK.

DEAR patient woman, o'er your children bending
  To leave a good-night kiss on rosy lips,
Or list the simple prayers to God ascending
  Ere slumber veil them in its soft eclipse, —
I wonder, do you dream that seraphs love you,
  And sometimes smooth the pathway for your feet;
That oft their silvery pinions float above you,
  When life is tangled and its cross-roads meet?

So wan and tired, the whole long day so busy;
  To laugh or weep, at times, you hardly know;
So many trifles make the poor brain dizzy,
  So many errands call you to and fro.
Small garments stitching, weaving fairy stories,
  And binding wounds and bearing little cares,
Your hours pass; unheeded all the glories
  Of that great world beyond your nursery stairs.

One schoolmate's pen has written words of beauty;
   Her poems sing themselves into the heart.
Another's brush has magic.   You have duty,
   No time to spare for poetry or art, —
But only time for training little fingers,
   And teaching youthful spirits to be true;
You know not with what famine woman lingers,
   With art alone to fill her, watching you.

And yet, I think you 'd rather keep the babies,
   Albeit their heads grow heavy on your arm,
Than have the poet's fair, enchanted may-bes, —
   The artist's visions, rich with dazzling charm.
Sweet are the troubles of the happy hours,
   For even in weariness your soul is blest;
And rich contentment all your being dowers,
   That yours is not a hushed and empty nest.

IN THE KING'S BANQUETING HOUSE.

I WALK on my way with the others, I toil at my daily
    task ;
I am sometimes weary and careworn, and sometimes I
    wear a mask,
And cover with smiles and sunshine a heart that is full of
    tears ;
And yet, and yet, there is joy divine, and it crowns my
    burdened years ;

For sometimes there comes a whisper in the silence of my
    soul :
" Rise up, my love, my fair one, and forget the sorrow and
    dole,
And come to the house of the banquet, and feast with the
    King to-day."
And oh ! when I hear the summons, is there aught except
    to obey?

And the look on his brow is loving, a brow that was worn
    and marred ;
And the hands I clasp with reverence, — ah me ! they are
    torn and scarred ;
And the voice that speaks is tender. " It is finished,"
    that dear voice said,
When on Calvary's mount for me, for me, he bowed his
    fainting head.

Oh, 't is sweet to sit at the banquet, a guest of the King
    divine ;
'T is sweet to taste the heavenly bread, and to drink the
    heavenly wine, —
To look away from the earth-cares, to lift the spirit above,
To sit in his shadow with great delight, under his banner
    of love.

And what if the way be dreary, and I sometimes think it
    long ?
There 's always, sooner or later, a bit of a cheery song.
And what if the clouds above me are sometimes thick and
    gray ?
There is never a cloud on the Mercy-seat, where I meet
    him day by day.

So I go on my way with the others, I am often weary and
  spent ;
But aye in my heart I am thankful, happy and well content ;
For oft in the early dawning, and oft at the fall of day,
He calls me in to the banquet, and what can I do but
  obey?

THE FAIRY'S GIFT.

OVER the little one's cradle
    The fairies were bending, to see
How like to a beautiful fairy
    A child of the earth could be.

"What shall we do for the baby?"
    Whispered the Elfin queen.
"I 'll give her the loveliest dimples,"
    Said one, "that ever were seen."

"I 'll kiss," said another softly,
    "Her feet so slender and small,
And ever on beautiful errands
    Their lightsome steps shall fall."

" Mine shall be fairer treasure :
   I 'll give her, for a spell,
A hand like pearl, with rosy tips,
   Like the inner side of a shell ;

" With a touch as soft as a zephyr's,
   The flaxen curls between,
I 'll dower thee royally, little one."
   Then spoke the Fairy Queen, —

" The years shall bring thee changes,
   But ever, in storm or shine,
The power of winning hearts, dear,
   And holding them fast, be thine."

A rustle as light as a rose-leaf's,
   That drops from a rose o'erblown,
And the silken wings of the fairies
   From cradle and babe were flown.

She grew into grace and beauty ;
   And the bright years, one by one,
Brought that to the soul of the maiden
   Which the peach wins from the sun.

She left her youth behind her,
  And the dead leaves round her fell,
The snow came down, and the winter wind,
  With many a moaning swell;

But she kept the gift of the Fairy —
  The beautiful gift — to the end;
And whenever her heart touched another
  She found the heart of a friend.

WASHINGTON'S BIRTHDAY.

NO rockets flamed in sudden fire,
    No ringing gladness rocked the spire,
No proud salute, o'er field and town,
Was loud each lesser sound to drown, —
When, on that morning long ago,
A fair young mother, spent and low,
Heard words so sweet: "God give you joy;
The baby is a splendid boy!"

Just words, as simple and as sweet
As ever fall in soft repeat,
Where, after weariness and strain,
And speechless ecstasy of pain,
In hall or hut, the mother waits,
So close to death's unfolding gates,
Till thrills her heart the solemn chord,
The gift exultant from the Lord,
And all her life o'erbrims with joy, —
Her man-child born, her baby boy.

The wide Virginia fields were green
With tender wheat in springing sheen ;
O'er mountain slopes and valleys fair
Hung violet mists in golden air ;
Coy sap was stirring in the trees,
Faint fragrance fluttered through the breeze,
And robin trills and bluebirds' notes
Came shrilling forth from merry throats ;
While hushed and happy in her joy
The mother looked upon her boy.

She dreamed not then of fateful strands
That yet should fill those tiny hands ;
Nor camp, nor foray, nor retreat,
Nor flag, nor march, nor stormy beat
Of forceful drum, was in her thought,
Her mind with gentle pleasure fraught.
Not hers to know that many an age
Would reap a sacred heritage
Because her child, her precious one,
Should be his country's noblest son.
No grand ambition marred the joy
She poured upon her baby boy.

To-day, from surf-washed shore to shore,
The deep-lipped guns in triumph roar;
The bells in stately music swing,
The sweet-voiced children laugh and sing;
From mast and fort the pennons fly,
The silken banners stream on high,
And homes and hearts are filled with mirth,
Remembering that baby's birth.

To-day, who gaze along the years,
The finished time of toils and tears,
That still in varying peace and strife
Have gone to make the nation's life, —
Who backward gaze must own the debt
We owe our holiest memory yet;
For all our best, bequeathed, begun,
We needs must honor Washington,
Still first among our good and great,
The grandest name that stars the state.

THE MINUET.

CLUSTERED like roses, the golden lights
    Shine on the polished and gleaming floor ;
Garlands are flung from the shadowy heights
    Of carven cornice and oaken door ;
Banners are draped on the stately walls,
    Tapestries flicker in faded grace,
And clear from the lifted gallery falls —
    Waking the glow in each happy face —
        The brilliant music, with rest and fret,
        And slow, sweet strains, for the minuet.

Bright as the blossoms that slip the sheath
    Of the folding calyx are maidens fair,
Their beauty and sparkle hid beneath
    Hoods that cover the crinkled hair.
Loosen the mantle, unclasp the shawl,
    Let ermine and sable be laid aside,

For the small feet tap at the tuneful call,
  And scarce can wait through the dance to glide.
    Loiter not now when they form the set
    For the courtly, dignified minuet.

The ladies are robed in such rich attire
  As well might ransom a captive king ;
There is flashing of jewels in lucent fire,
  There is diamond lustre in brooch and ring ;
Perfumes of Araby scent the air,
  Flutter the fans, and the blushes rise
To cheeks whose velvety dimples wear
  The pale pink flush of the dawning skies.
    Who that hath seen it can e'er forget
    The radiant charm of the minuet?

The men who bow with such gallant pride,
  Who utter such compliments, sweet and low,
Are men who in many a list have tried
  The crossing lance with the valiant foe :
The plumes that they doff with such knightly ease
  Have swept the field in a whirl of steel,
With the sword's swift rush, like the sound of seas,
  With mail-clad breast and a spur at heel ;
    But the triumphs of war their hearts forget
    When they lead the fair in the minuet.

Here statesmen keen at the council board,
    Skilled and shrewd in the deep debate,
Are bland as the breezes of summer, stored
    With the honey of lilies at evening late.
The white head bends to the golden curls,
    The grave lips stoop to the snowy hand,
And suave petitions are dropped like pearls
    By voices used unto stern command, —
        Dame and demoiselle queening yet
        The formal grace of the minuet.

Touched with enchantment is love's young dream,
    Wreathing its fancy in glance and smile ;
Glamor and rapture and bliss outbeam
    From eyes that are pure of the worldling's guile.
Sanguine and eager and strong of soul
    Is the lad in his nobleness, brave and high, —
Lifted from aught that could hold control
    Unworthy the lady, so sweet and shy,
        Whose finger-tips with his own are met
        In the courteous, reticent minuet.

Pause we now ere we turn the page ;
    Fleet let the beautiful pageant pass, —
Glimpse of the pomp of a splendid age,
    Blooming here as in magic glass.

Swift through the waltz as we flit along,
   Something we've lost of the languid grace,
Subtle and soft as remembered song,
   Which thrills in the airy and pictured space,
     Where the music throbs and the dance is set, —
     The proud, the leisurely minuet.

THE CHRISTMAS BALL: 1780.

Suggested by a Picture.

SCINTILLANT stars in the sky's blue height,
   Frost in the breath of the keen, cold night,
Ice that rings to the skater's heel,
River and lake as firm as steel;
Steeds that with flying feet keep time
To the merry, merry sleigh-bells' chime;
A world of music, a world of snow,
A world of fun, and away they go,
Beautiful, courtly, brave, and bright, —
Maiden, matron, squire, and knight,
Bloom of the cottage, and pride of the hall,
To dance till dawn at the Christmas Ball.

Splendid the rooms in vista seen,
Wreathed with the wealth of the evergreen.
Spice of the forest, exquisite, fine,
Floats aromatic from cedar and pine.
Glossy the white of the mistletoe,
And the holly is vivid in scarlet show.
Floods of the mellowest lustre fall
From bowery ceiling and garlanded wall.

Floors are smooth to the tripping feet,
Blithe hearts thrill with a quicker beat,
As resonant voices the measures call,
And the glad hours flit at the Christmas Ball.

Gray old fiddler with solemn face,
Wielding the bow with a master's grace,
Harper, whose notes drop liquid sweet,
As the sound of a brooklet's tinkling feet,
You 're weaving in with the jocund tunes
Harmonies blissful and magic runes ;
For eyes meet eyes in electric glance
As the figures change in the mazy dance.
There are whispered questions and soft replies,
There is shy surrender to love's surprise,
And by and by there 'll be priest and ring,
And the wedding march, and the hearts that cling,
Semper fidelis, whate'er befall,
Pledged this eve at the Christmas Ball.

Seventeen-eighty !   A hundred years
Have sped, with their mingled smiles and tears,
Since these ladies rustled in stiff brocade,
These gentlemen bowed, and these pipers played.

" Promenade all," and the century 's past,
We 're rounding the hundredth year at last.
The fair and brave of that vanished day
Like shadows and dreams have gone their way.
The young grew old, and the gay grew tired,
Till nothing so much their thoughts desired
As a tranquil place to lie down and sleep,
Where the bed was low and the rest was deep.
The pearls, the rubies, the yellow lace,
Descended oft, with a lovely face,
To some bright girl who was proud of all
That grandma had worn at *her* Christmas Ball.

And ever at Christmas the joy-bells ring,
The tapers shine and the children sing ;
Ever at Christmas the tidal mirth
Sweeps in its fulness over the earth.
Roses and lilies the century through
Make summer at Christmas when love is true —
The dear new love that is pure as gold,
The strong, tried love that is dear as old.
Oh, swift steeds bound o'er the powdery snow,
Oh, blithe hearts beat as away we go.
Eighteen-eighty ! The sweet notes fall,
And the dancers meet at the Christmas Ball.

A LOST PEARL.

I DO not know where I lost it,
    For it slipped from a broken string,
And far and away from my sight to-day,
    It lies, a neglected thing.

Or worse, since it may be another
    Is wearing my pearl of price,
And the gem that was mine, with its lucent shine,
    May be set in some strange device.

I do not know when I lost it;
    It was just as the dawning burst
Through the crystalline bars of the lingering stars,
    That with sorrow I missed it first.

Perhaps in an opaline twilight,
    Perhaps when the moonbeams lay,
With their delicate quiver o'er field and river,
    And night was fairer than day.

I never dreamed half how precious
   Was my beautiful pearl to me,
Till the grief of its loss, a heavy cross,
   I bore over land and sea.

You marvel? You do not divine it?
   I have lost what I could not lend,
What I 'll mourn while I live ; for no art can give
   To my heart the lost heart of my friend.

A SEAFOG.

UP from the sea came a chill gray mist,
    Between midnight hour and morn.
The stars on high that were biding tryst
    From watching eyes were borne ;
And the green fields, late by the sunlight kissed,
    In the darkness lay forlorn.

There seemed no hope in the shrouded sky,
    No help in the hills remote ;
'T was as if no more from the greenwood nigh,
    Should the song of the robin float ;
Nor the roses bloom, nor the young birds fly,
    Nor the oriole sound a note.

For up from the sea came that mist of death,
    So vague, so wan, so white ;

A Seafog.

The sea of trouble and woe, and faith
   Grew timorous at the sight,
And love sank down, at the shivering breath
   Of a cruel and creeping blight.

That hour of waiting, how slowly it wore
   Its heart-beats dull away !
Distant and cold seemed the shining shore
   Of the beautiful yesterday,
While wearily life its burden bore
   Along the sorrowful way.

Fair in the East, lo ! a line of light
   Pulsed and quivered and broke.
God's finger moved in its gentle might,
   God's silence tenderly spoke.
The seafog lifted !   The fears took flight !
   The soul from its trance awoke.

Ah ! whence shall the wrecked on the perilous reef
   Of doubts, that like mists arise,
Find the flash of the lances that bring relief,
   If not in the morning skies ?
And where shall they cry, through their utter grief,
   Except unto Paradise ?

The gloom will pass, and the glory dawn,
   When the birds begin to sing,
When the murk of the night is swiftly gone,
   In the day's rich blossoming,
And garments of praise the soul puts on
   As it bows to its gracious King.